One Magical Summer

BY
KAREN CLOW

Bloomington, IN Milton Keynes, UK

authorHOUSE®

AuthorHouse™
1663 Liberty Drive, Suite 200
Bloomington, IN 47403
www.authorhouse.com
Phone: 1-800-839-8640

AuthorHouse™ UK Ltd.
500 Avebury Boulevard
Central Milton Keynes, MK9 2BE
www.authorhouse.co.uk
Phone: 08001974150

First published by AuthorHouse 5/2/2007

ISBN: 978-1-4259-9083-1 (sc)

Printed in the United States of America
Bloomington, Indiana

This book is printed on acid-free paper.

About the Author

KAREN CLOW was born in East Sussex where she has lived all her life. She has three grown up daughters and two grandchildren. She and her husband Pete are full time foster carers. She has been writing short stories for many years, mainly for her own children in their early years.

One Magical Summer is her first published work, and is dedicated to her beloved mum Mickey who sadly passed away in 2005. Her adored dad Jim had sadly passed away four years earlier and it was their dearest wish to see Karen's work published. She would also like to dedicate this book to her family for their unstinting love, faith and encouragement.

Acknowledgments

I would like to express my heartfelt thanks to my lifelong friend Janet, without whose help this book would not have been published.

Thanks also, to my daughter Ruth, who did the illustrations and my wonderful grandchildren, Leoni and Maddison for helping to inspire me.

Last but not least, my wonderful niece Madeline, whose cheeky personality reminds me of fairies, imps elves and all manner of magical beings.

CHAPTER ONE

Aunt Clara's Letter

Jamie sat with his nose pressed against the window. He had been waiting for an hour for the mailman to arrive. The family was expecting a letter from England, from Aunt Clara to be more precise. "He's here", shouted Jamie as he rushed past his mother. "Slow down", she called but he was already out the door. The mail man had barely placed the mail in the box before Jamie had scooped it up, taking the steps up to the house two at a time. "It's here mum, it's here!" "Perhaps we should wait till your dad and sister get home." "No mum, please open it now I cannot wait another minute!" "Ok then Jamie but remember, it may not say what you're hoping to hear." Slowly she began to read the letter, stopping every few seconds to glance at Jamie. The poor lad could hardly contain himself. "Well mum can we? What has aunt Clara said?" "It would seem that Aunt Clara is as keen as you and your sister." "YIPPEE", shouted Jamie. "So we can go then?" "Let's calm down; we'll discus it with your father later." "He will let us go mum, won't he?" "Oh I expect so son but there is a lot to consider. Yours and your sister's safety would definitely have to be a major consideration. After all England is a long way from America and neither of you have ever travelled alone." "Mum you know we would be fine, anyway I'll take care of Maddy." "Oh I'm sure you would Jamie but who would take care of you?" They both started laughing.

The porch door slammed. "Hi Sally, we're home." Jamie rushed to meet his dad and Maddy, unable to hold back his excitement. He began telling them that Aunt Clara's letter had arrived and that she would love it if the twins went to stay with her in England. Maddy started jumping up and down with excitement, her voice getting louder and louder, trying to make herself heard above Jamie. Neither one of them had noticed Sally appear, well not until she shouted to the pair of them to calm down! Within an instant there was silence. "Thank God for that", said John, "for a moment there I thought I was in a madhouse." "Stressful day at work dear?" asked Sally with a grin. "Oh and thanks for picking Maddy up from dance class, I just couldn't face that drive on the freeway." "No problem. I had a late lunch with a client, a very boring client. I was glad for an excuse to get away, although I did miss out on coffee." "Ok John I can take a hint, shall we have coffee in the lounge?" "Yeah, that would be great."

The twins sat patiently waiting while John and Sally chatted about their day. Jamie began tapping his fingers along the arm of the chair. He was a natural born fidget; he always had to do everything there and then. Patience was certainly not his strong point. His twin sister Maddy however, seemed to have more than her fair share. She was the calmer one, the thinker; always seemed to wait until exactly the right moment before opening her mouth, especially where John was concerned. She could wrap him around her little finger. She was a real daddies' girl. The twins were identical in looks, even down to a small birth mark just below the knuckle on their index finger. Sally bore exactly the same mark, a small half moon inside a circle in exactly the same place. This seemed to be the only feature they inherited from Sally. They had their father's piercing blue eyes and ash blonde hair although Maddy preferred hers long. They both shared a love of animals and despite them being only eleven years old, they were already certain that they wanted to be veterinarians when they left college. Fortunately, Sally shared their love for animals and since they were babies she had encouraged them to learn more about the subject. She herself had been raised in the English countryside on a small farm. She would probably never have left had she not had met John, a dashing young lawyer, during a holiday to the States some twenty years earlier.

Jamie couldn't stand it any longer. He had waited for thirty minutes for Sally to mention the letter from Aunt Clara, "MUM can we please ask dad about the holiday?" John looked towards Jamie with a frown. "It's very rude to interrupt son." "Sorry dad, but we've been waiting for ages," "Yes we appreciate that son, but your mother and I had more important things to discuss. However, perhaps I should read Aunt Clara's letter and make a decision so that you two can leave us in peace." "Thanks dad," smiled Maddy. The few seconds it took John to read the letter seemed like an eternity to the twins. Finally he put the letter down and, glancing at Sally, said "Well Sal what do you think?" She paused for a moment before answering. " Well I know Clara would love to have them stay and I've absolutely no doubt that she will take wonderful care of them, so providing we can ensure that the travel arrangements are completely safe, I don't really see any problems but it's up to you." "OH please dad, we promise we'll be really careful and we'll be really good for Aunt Clara." "Is that a real promise?" Yes dad," said Maddy, "we promise." "Then in that case I suppose we had better make the arrangements." "YES!" shouted Jamie, punching the air, "we are going to England!"

CHAPTER TWO

The Journey

"Now make sure you put your passports somewhere safe," ordered John in a very firm voice. "Don't talk to strangers and under no circumstances leave the airport with anyone but Aunt Clara." "Yes dad we know, you've told us a thousand times, we won't go with anyone but Aunt Clara." "Remember to ring us from the airport when you meet Clara. We'll expect a phone call every three days whilst you are away." "Ok dad we know, every three days." "We wouldn't have this problem if your Aunt Clara had a phone," muttered John. "It's just the way she is", said Sally. "Every time I write to her, I beg her to get one but she won't hear of it. You know how stubborn she is." "Stubborn isn't the word for it. I sometimes wonder if your sister realises that we are living in the twenty first century. In fact, sometimes I actually think she's caught in a time warp." "Oh John, don't be so unkind, you really like Clara. She's just a little eccentric that's all!" Maddy tugged at John's arm. "Dad they have just announced our flight, we need to board the plane."

John and Sally watched as the twins boarded. As the plane began to taxi along the runway they were waving frantically at the two tiny figures in the distance, hoping they were the twins. On board the plane, Janet the stewardess asked the twins if they would like anything from the trolley. Jamie decided on a can of coke, while Maddy opted for the healthier option of spring water. Janet chatted to the twins about their trip to England. They told her about Aunt Clara and how their dad thought she was a bit eccentric. "Why does he think that?" Jamie explained that Aunt Clara lived in a small village in Kent; her nearest neighbour being about a mile away. She didn't have a telephone or a television and there was only one shop and a post office. "Oh how awful," said Janet, "won't you kids be bored?" "No way!" exclaimed Jamie. "It's great at Aunt Clara's; she takes us on country rambles, lets us help bake bread and make jams, all that sort of stuff." "Don't forget about the herbs and stuff," said Maddy. "What do you mean, herbs and stuff?" asked a rather puzzled Janet. Jamie, as always, was keen to explain. "She makes medicine from herbs and plants, that sort of thing." "Really?" "Oh yes!" stated Maddy, "everyone in the village goes to her when they have something wrong and sometimes when they're really sick, Aunt Clara goes to their homes." "Well, it certainly sounds like you kids will be having a lot of fun this summer." "We will, especially without mum and dad. They usually take us but dad cannot get away this year, so Aunt Clara will be able to show us how to do things. Mum always says no when she's there. She always tells Aunt Clara that we're too young to understand. Not this year though, it will just be us and Aunt Clara for six whole weeks." Janet suggested that the twins put on the headphones as there was a good film about to start. "If you need anything just let me know. We'll be in England before you know it." They thanked her for her help before settling down to watch the movie. It was Robin Hood Prince of Thieves, a particular favourite of Jamie's, Kevin Costner being one of his favourite actors. Maddy decided to read her book, as well as watch the movie, although she was not particularly interested in either.

As the plane landed, the twins strained their eyes trying to spy Aunt Clara through the huge glass windows of the airport lounge area. "Can you see her Maddy?" asked Jamie. "No but I would imagine she will be waiting as we come through the barrier after customs have checked us out." Janet told the twins that she would accompany them to the airport lounge. "We'll be fine," said Jamie. "Oh I'm sure you will," answered Janet, " it's just that it's the airlines policy that children travelling alone are accompanied by a member of staff; not that I think you two really need looking after but just in case your Aunt Clara's been held up or anything." As the three of them passed through customs Maddy excitedly stated that she could see Aunt Clara waiting at the end of the corridor. The twins began waving frantically. "Aunt Clara!" shouted Jamie. Janet watched as a small plump woman with grey streaked hair pulled tight in an old fashioned bun on top of her head, a pair of school mistress type spectacles resting on the end of her nose, wearing a long knitted cardigan which all but hid the plaid skirt and blouse she was wearing underneath, began to wave back at the twins. Janet could not help but think to herself that indeed this lady did look a trifle eccentric, although as they approached she noticed what a kindly face Clara had and that there was something very warm and inviting about her. The twins rushed through the crowd of passengers. Jamie launched himself at Aunt Clara, almost sending her toppling backwards with the impact. She steadied herself just in time to throw her arms around him. He was quickly followed by Maddy. "It's so wonderful to see you both!" exclaimed Clara. "My word how you've both grown, can it really be a year since I've seen you?" Janet interrupted the reunion. She introduced herself to Clara holding out her hand. "I'm terribly sorry my dear," said Clara as she shook her hand. "Thank you for looking after them for me." "It was my pleasure," replied Janet, "they have entertained me with their stories about you." Clara blushed. "Oh dear, I hope they haven't overdone it!" she chuckled." "No, not at all! It was all very interesting but now I must leave you all and wish you the best holiday ever because, unfortunately, I have to get back to work." Clara offered her hand again only this time she seemed to grip Janet's hand more firmly than before. As she did so, she leaned towards her and in a quiet voice told Janet not to worry about Cynthia, because everything would soon be fine and that in no time at all, she would be fit and well again. As the twins walked off with Aunt Clara they looked back to wave at Janet, who, for some unknown reason, appeared to be oblivious to them. She was just standing there with a puzzled look on her face. "I have a car waiting for us," Aunt Clara told them. "Didn't you drive?" asked Maddy. "Good heavens no!" replied Aunt Clara. "I couldn't possibly drive in all the traffic; far too many cars on the road, people in such a hurry to get everywhere. I'll stick to driving in the village, nice and slow, just how I like it. A good friend of mine offered to drive, ah there he is now." The twins glanced over to where Aunt Clara was pointing. A large built man with bushy sideburns and a handle bar moustache, reaching right out to the side of his face, was waving his hand at Aunt Clara. He was driving a dusty old pickup truck which had a large dent in the wing. Jamie told Aunt Clara that he looked like a hillbilly. Fortunately, he did not hear what Jamie called him and Aunt Clara quickly corrected her young nephew by explaining that her friend Tom was in fact a pig farmer, not to mention her good friend and neighbour.

As they approached the truck Clara introduced them to Tom "Don't 'spose you two remember me do ya?" The twins shook their heads. "Well taz been a long time since I've seen ya both, prob'ly a year or two ago." The twins tried hard not to giggle at the way Tom spoke. If their mum had been there she would have said he was an old country yokel. Back home in the States she would often mimic the way the English farm yokels talked, making the twins laugh. The three of them squeezed into the front of Tom's truck. It wasn't long before they were on the way back to Kent, looking out of the truck window. Maddy could understand why her mum referred to Kent as the Garden of England. She watched as they drove past endless fields of cows and sheep; the English countryside was indeed a beautiful place, not a bit like New York with its huge concrete tower blocks and endless shopping malls. The air in England even smelled better, clean and fresh. Maddy thought to herself that perhaps she could become a vet in England one day. She snapped out of her lovely daydream when the truck started bouncing up and down. Jamie, who had dozed off, woke up suddenly. The cobbled road they where driving along never seemed this rough when their dad drove a hire car. They both recognised it as the rough track that led up to Aunt Clara's cottage. It was just as it had been the last time the twins were there. A white picket fence enclosed the pretty front garden. It was full of beautiful plants and flowers, all different sizes and colours, gently swaying in harmony in the light evening breeze. Maddy noticed the wonderful aroma as she jumped down from the truck. It was almost as if someone was spraying perfume into the evening air. "Tom, would you like to come in for a cup of tea?" "I won't thank ye all the same Clara, I best be gittin' back to me pigs, they'll be wantin' their supper." "As you wish Tom but, before you go, how much do I owe you for today?" "Don't be daft, you don't owe me nowt. It was my pleasure to do something for you for a change."

11

"But Tom I insist!" said Clara. "I tell ya wot, hows about ya making me some of that fine jam and marmalade you're famous for?" "Consider it done; I'll have it to you by the end of the week." "Cheerio," called Tom, "be good for Clara." They waited until his truck was out of sight before going inside.

CHAPTER THREE

Settling In

Once inside Aunt Clara suggested that they should have a nice cup of tea before unpacking. The kettle began to whistle. "Ah lovely," said Aunt Clara "a nice cup of tea coming up!" She asked Maddy to put out some cups, which were housed on a rack just above the kitchen sink. As the three of them sat drinking tea, Jamie noticed that Aunt Clara had the very same birth mark as them. He asked her if everyone from their family had one. Hesitating for a moment, Aunt Clara explained that, as far as she could remember, all the relatives on her mother's side of the family had the mark, but not her father or any of his siblings. Maddy interrupted, "don't you think that's weird Aunt Clara?" she asked. "Not really my dear," said Clara; I like to think of it as something special, you know, a bit different that's all." "What do you mean Aunt Clara, something special?" questioned Jamie. "Aunt Clara smiled at him. "All in good time my dear boy, all in good time." Maddy looked intrigued. "What do you mean Aunt Clara?" she asked. "It's getting late, we're all tired, we'll talk about it tomorrow." said Clara," Now you two run along upstairs and sort out your night wear, we can unpack tomorrow. I'll just do us a bit of supper."

Jamie and Maddy carried their suitcases up to the bedroom. It was exactly the same as the last time they had been there. Crisp white cotton sheets with hand stitched patchwork quilts on the beds, a jug of water and two glasses on a small tray placed on the small bedside cabinet between the two beds. There was a large old fashioned wardrobe and a matching chest of drawers with a lovely basket of dried flowers sitting on the top. In fact you would say the room was typical of a country cottage, a far cry from the luxurious surroundings that the twins were accustomed to back in New York. Their parents seemed to have every modern appliance known to man, they had a cleaner who came in five days a week, and they ate out in restaurants more often than not, usually when John or Sally had to work late. John was a lawyer in a very prestigious law firm, the clients being very rich and some very famous. Sally was a doctor; she worked in the emergency department. She was always ringing Debbie the child minder, asking if she could stay later with the twins because there had been a major traffic accident or such like. Debbie was always willing to help out; she was trying to put herself through medical school, so the extra money was always needed. Sally would often help her with her studies. She was far more than a sitter, she was regarded as family. Sally thought very well of her, they were more like best friends. Very often, John and Sally would pay Debbie to help out even if the twins were at school. Debbie would protest that she wasn't really needed, although she knew that it was Sally's way of helping her out, as money was always tight. However, the one true thing they both shared was their passion for their chosen career, and although Debbie was only twenty one and a first year medical student, Sally could already see that Debbie would make a fine doctor. Sally loved her work; she would often go in to work on her day off because of staff shortages. Yes, life in the English countryside was indeed a far cry from New York, but the twins seemed to fit right in.

There was no doubt they both loved spending time with Aunt Clara, she was indeed a very fascinating lady. Although very different from Sally, there was something very special about her. "Supper's ready," called Clara.

The twins dashed off down the stairs "Coming!" The table was laden with sandwiches and cakes, "tuck in." The twins didn't need telling twice. Aunt Clara watched in amazement as Jamie filled his plate with endless supplies of food. "I see the country air has given you a healthy appetite young Jamie." "He always eats like that," said Maddy, "mum says he's got hollow legs, that's why he doesn't get fat". Aunt Clara chuckled. They chatted about the flight and things back in America. Jamie thought it was funny that when they had phoned home to confirm their safe arrival, it was the middle of the night and that John and Sally were probably fast asleep. Maddy asked Aunt Clara what she had said to Janet the air hostess about someone called Cynthia. Aunt Clara looked slightly taken aback. "Well my dear, I just knew, when I shook her hand, that she was very worried about somebody called Cynthia, her sister I believe." "How did you know?" enquired Jamie. "Oh I just get feelings about things that's all. Hopefully, while you two are here, I can explain some things to you." "Things? What sort of things?" "All sorts of things, but it's getting late now and you two need some rest or you'll be fit for nothing tomorrow, so let's have you off to bed now. We can catch up on everything tomorrow." "Will you come to say goodnight?" asked Maddy. "Of course, my dear. I'll just clear away these dishes while you two get ready for bed." "Can I ask you something Aunt Clara?" "Of course Maddy, what is it?" "Will Cynthia really be alright?" "Most definitely!" stated

Aunt Clara in a positive voice. "That's good. Janet was so nice to us."

Once in the bedroom the twins were soon ready for bed. Jamie looked out of the window. "Crikey!" he exclaimed. "I had forgotten how dark it gets in the country, I can't see a thing." Maddy peered out to investigate. "Blimey! Its pitch black, I can't see anything. All I can hear are the crickets." The twins snuggled back down into their beds. Maddy put her headphones on to listen to her music CDs, while Jamie listened to the crickets. In some strange way, he imagined that they were actually speaking a secret language. For a brief moment he thought he could actually understand what they were saying. Aunt Clara appeared in the doorway. "Are you two settled in?" "I am," replied Jamie, his sister being unaware of Clara's presence. Jamie soon remedied that by leaning over and poking her. "Ouch!" complained Maddy." "Sorry Aunt Clara, I never heard you come in." "I don't suppose you did with all that din." "They're called the Black Eyed Peas and they're one of my favourite bands" said Maddy. "The Black Eyed Peas! Whatever sort of a name is that?" "Oh they're great Aunt Clara; you should listen to them some time." "Perhaps I will one day, but now I think you two should be getting some sleep, the morning will come round very quickly. Can I get either of you anything before I go?" "We're fine, thank you." "Well in that case I'll bid you both good night, sleep well, see you in the morning." "Good night Aunt Clara."

The morning alarm was sounded by Clara's trusty cockerel Winston. Maddy woke with a start. "What on earth is that?" she mumbled. She looked over to Jamie's bed hoping he could enlighten her as to the noise, but it came as no surprise to her to find him still fast asleep. "Jamie, wake up!" He began to stir. "What's that noise?" Straining to open his eyes, "noise what noise?" "Cock-a-doodle-doo" sang Winston "That noise," said Maddy. "That's Winston," said Jamie, "don't you remember him, he's Aunt Clara's cockerel, damn bird!" Suddenly, Jamie was distracted from Winston by the most glorious smell. "Breakfast! Come on Maddy, Aunt Clara's cooking." Before Maddy was out of her bed, Jamie was already making his way down the stairs. "Good morning Jamie, where's your sister?" asked Aunt Clara. "I'm here" "Oh good morning Maddy, I hope you both slept well?" "We did, it was Winston who woke us up." "Yes, my dear Winston, he's better than any alarm clock. Five o'clock on the dot every morning." "FIVE O'CLOCK!" exclaimed the twins in unison. "Why would any sane person want to get up at 5 o'clock?" asked Jamie. Aunt Clara smiled. "We country folk like to rise early so as we don't miss anything important." Jamie looked baffled; he asked Aunt Clara what could possibly be missed this early in the morning. "Well there's the fairy folk for instance. You'll rarely catch a fairy out after six o'clock, too dangerous for them" The twins laughed. "I take it that you two don't believe in fairies any more?" "Of course not!" said Maddy. "When we were little, we loved your stories about the fairies, but we're grown up now, so we know they're not real" "Oh you do, do you?" said Clara."Well, what if I told you that my stories about fairies were actually true and that King Peteron and his family really exist?" "Aunt Clara, we know you're just teasing us." said Maddy. "On the contrary my dear, I'm telling you the truth." Both Maddy and Jamie realised that Aunt Clara did indeed seem to be telling the truth. They looked at one another. Was this simply another tale or were there really fairies? Clara broke the silence. "Ok then Jamie, just pretend that you believe my stories. Who would be your favourite fairy?" Without hesitation, Jamie said "Wickit." "Why him?" "Because he's funny, always getting into trouble and stuff." "What about you Maddy, who is your favourite?" "I'm not sure, probably one of the princesses." "Which one?" "Umm ... I think it would be Princess Melissa." "Why her?" "Because she's clever and beautiful and is not afraid to make her own decisions." "I'm pleased to know that you two have listened to my so called stories, but we'll have to continue this conversation in a moment, because I do believe breakfast is ready. I assume you two are ready to eat?" "Sure are," beamed Jamie.

Aunt Clara placed a full English breakfast in front of the twins; egg, bacon, sausage, tomatoes and mushrooms filled their plates. In the centre of the table, Clara placed a plate of hot toast. Jars of home made jam and marmalade completed the feast. "WOW," said Jamie "this beats mum's breakfast hands down." Clara chuckled. "Tuck in you two, don't let it get cold, I'll pour the tea unless you two would prefer something else." Their mouths too full to answer Aunt Clara, they nodded to express their approval of tea. Finishing the last scrap of sausage from his plate, "I'm stuffed" sighed Jamie. "Me too," echoed Maddy. "That was lovely Aunt Clara; I wish mum could cook like you." "Well your mother has other talents, like the way she heals people and the way she cares for her family. We can't all be good at the same things." "You heal people too Aunt Clara," stated Maddy "and you tell the most wonderful stories." "So you still believe they're only stories?" "There can't really be fairies can there?" asked Jamie. "Absolutely my dear boy!" "Truly Aunt Clara, you're not just teasing us are you?" "No Jamie I'm not teasing you, allow me to explain.

Many years ago, centuries in fact, fairies lived in harmony with us. Most humans simply accepted them for what they were. However, there where some people who feared them because they were known to have magical powers and through their ignorance and fear, they all but wiped out these beautiful creatures." "Why would anyone want to hurt them Aunt Clara?" "People often fear what they don't understand, it's the same today. Anyway, they were hunted down, some were captured, others were killed but thankfully some escaped into the forests. It was there that they began to rebuild their numbers, but their fear of humans made them stay hidden, only coming out when it was safe, although there were some humans who defended the fairy folk, warning them of danger and helping them to rebuild their lives. These people became known as watchers and for generations, they have watched over the fairy folk. Because of their kindness, the fairies saw fit to reward them with certain gifts." "Gifts? What sort of gifts?" asked Jamie. "Special gifts, for instance the gift of healing; also the gift of magic." "MAGIC!" stuttered Jamie, "can you do magic?" "Yes a little, although I'm not really that good at it, your mother was always better at it than me." "Maddy stared at Clara. "Aunt Clara, are you telling us that mum's a witch?" "I suppose I am Maddy; actually she was quite an accomplished witch in her younger days." "NO WAY," said Jamie, "this is definitely a wind up, we've never seen mum do any magic." "That's because your mother decided to leave that all behind her when she met your dad, but there is no doubt in my mind that should your mum ever be called upon by the fairies, she would not hesitate, as a watcher, to help them." "Are you a watcher Aunt Clara?" asked Maddy. "Yes my dear, as are you and your brother," "OK Aunt Clara, if that's true then why has mum never told us?" queried Jamie. "Quite simply my dear, that's why you're both here. Your mother would never have told you, had she not have noticed certain things." "What things?" "Well, for instance Jamie, when you were lying in bed last night did you not think that the crickets were talking in a secret language? And you Maddy, back in America a few months ago, did you not tell Sally that you had dreamt about a fire at the hospital? Sally told me that two days after your dream there was indeed such a fire." "She never told us," said Jamie. "Exactly! That's why you're here now, so I can explain everything to you. In fact Jamie, you were quite right about the crickets, they do have their own language. Sally knew you were both blessed, from the day you came into this world, by the birth mark you both have on your finger. Only watchers are born with this mark. It is given to all watchers by Nanamic." "I remember her from your stories." said Maddy. "She's the oldest and wisest fairy of them all!" "I'm glad you remember her, she's very special," said Clara, "anyway, it was her way of letting the fairy folk know who they could trust. I suppose you could say it's your birthright, I'll tell you more about all these things later on, but now I think you should both wash and dress and sort your luggage out, we have a busy day ahead of us."

The twins rummaged through their cases looking for their toilet bags and toothbrushes. "I'll use the bathroom first," said Maddy. "Fine," replied Jamie, who was busy looking out of the window. "What are you looking at?" "Nothing." Jamie listened at the window. He could hear the sound of the crickets, he had never really noticed them before but now, for some strange reason, he seemed to hear them with perfect clarity, even to the point where he thought he could understand what they were saying. In his mind, the funny little sounds they made actually appeared to be a language that he understood. "Bathroom's free," said Maddy as she entered the bedroom. "God, you made me jump!" snapped Jamie. "SORRY," said a rather put out Maddy. Within minutes she was dressed and packing her clothes neatly into the drawers and wardrobe. She could hear Aunt Clara's footsteps climbing the stairs. "Where's Jamie?" asked Clara. "He's still in the bathroom." No sooner had the words come out of her mouth when Jamie rushed past Aunt Clara and dived onto his bed. "Steady," said Aunt Clara, "these old beds won't take much of that sort of treatment!" "Mum's always telling him off for doing that at home," said Maddy. "I don't doubt it," chuckled Clara. "When you're dressed and unpacked, come downstairs then we'll finish our conversation about watchers and the fairy folk. "I'm ready," boasted Maddy. "Good," said Clara," then you can help me pack away the dishes and we'll make a fresh pot of tea while we wait for Jamie to join us."

CHAPTER FOUR

Talking to Fairy Folk

Within no time at all the three of them were sitting round the table. Aunt Clara poured the tea; the twins sat silently waiting for Clara to say something. "I can only assume that your mother has never mentioned anything to you." They shook their heads. "Didn't think so, that's so typical of Sally, she always left the hardest things to me. I've often thought that one of the reasons she moved to America was to try and live a normal life. Well that and the fact that she was madly in love with your father; although I did explain to her at the time that it wouldn't change anything and of course I was right. That's why you two are here. Still, you would have to be told sooner or later so I suppose now is as good a time as any. I think the best place to start is with the fairy folk." "Have you ever seen one, Aunt Clara?" "Thousands of times; when your mother and I were children they would often come to see us." "Do they still come now?" "Well of course they do, we help each other." "What do you mean, help each other?" "If you two stop asking questions I will explain everything to you." "Will we get to meet any fairies Aunt Clara?"

"Oh for sure." "Will we be able to do magic?" asked a rather eager Jamie. "Yes, I will teach you as much as I can, but most of it will come naturally to you both, in time." Maddy interrupted, "Aunt Clara, is this really all true or are you just teasing us?" "Sally warned me that you would be the more sceptical of the two Maddy, but I suppose under the circumstances, no one could blame you." "I believe you Aunt Clara!" piped Jamie. "Well thank you dear, but your sister obviously needs proof, so I suppose I could give you a small demonstration."

The twins watched as Aunt Clara pointed at the tea tray. To their amazement, the milk jug rose into the air, travelled by itself over to Aunt Clara's cup, and then as if being guided by an invisible hand, slowly poured the milk into Clara's cup. Next came the tea pot, followed swiftly by two sugar lumps. Neither one of the twins moved; they were totally stunned by what they had just seen. Aunt Clara picked up the cup and sipped the tea, then peering over her tiny glasses, looked at Maddy and asked, "Was that good enough?" Maddy simply nodded her head, her beautiful blue eyes opened wide and her mouth slightly ajar. "Good," said Clara, "then shall we continue?"

The twins listened as Clara told them about fairy magic and such like, pausing only to ask was there anything either of them would like to know. By this time, the twins had regained their senses and were absolutely bursting with questions. Jamie wanted to know why the fairies still needed the help of humans if no one could see them. "Well my dear boy, unfortunately, it's not only humans who pose a threat to them, they have other enemies." "Like what?" "Well for starters there are elves, goblins, gnomes and trolls, but by far the nastiest are the Bawllows." "Bawllows," said Jamie, "what on earth are Bawllows?" "Well might you ask my dear, they are fairies who have gone bad. Just like humans, they wanted all the power. They even broke the sacred law and killed other fairies, a crime which is unforgivable and the punishment for such a crime is banishment, never again to be allowed to live amongst their own kind. So, many of them banded together and they sought the help of evil sorcerers, who in return for information about fairies and their powers, granted them safety.

They also taught them some of the blackest magic, but they paid a price for this and their once beautiful bodies became twisted and grotesque as the evil engulfed them. They have been known to kidnap fairy babies, to try to take their powers and regain their beauty. One thing is for sure, if ever you meet one, never ever look into their eyes. If you do, they will control you." "Have you ever seen one Aunt Clara?" "Unfortunately, yes. It was many years ago when I was just a young girl about your age. I was searching in the woods with your mother for the fairy Princess Michelalena, who had wandered out from the safety of her village. Her parents, Queen Kaznia and King Peteron where frantic with worry and because it was in the late afternoon, just before dusk, they feared for her life, as that is the time when the Bawllows are at their most dangerous." "What happened

Aunt Clara? Did you find the princess?" "Yes, thank God, but sadly, at a terrible price!" "What happened?" "Well, that particular afternoon the worst and most powerful of Bawllows, a male called Dragonscott, was aware that the princess was alone in the woods. We still believe to this day that he enchanted her, which is why she left the safety of her village. He had taken on the form of a handsome fairy; oh did I tell you they could change shape and form?" said Clara. "No" echoed the twins. "Well they can, but fortunately, only for short periods. On this particular day he had done just that and my oh my, was he handsome! It's no wonder that the princess fell for him, although she herself is a rare beauty, the kindest sweetest fairy you could ever wish to lay eyes on. Anyway, that terrible day, your mother, who was about five at the time and I, found Princess Michelalena talking to Dragonscott, although we had no idea who or what he was; we simply thought he was another fairy who had been searching for the princess and had subsequently found her. We never doubted him for one minute when he told us that he would return with her to the village.

As the princess seemed happy to be with him I never questioned it. To this very day I still feel responsible for what happened. Your mother was too young to understand but I should have known." Maddy and Jamie noticed a tear running down Clara's cheek. Maddy gently squeezed Clara's hand. "Don't cry, tell us what happened." Taking her handkerchief and wiping her eyes from under her glasses Aunt Clara continued. "As

27

we headed back to our cottage we met Queen Kaznia, who by now was frantic with worry. I explained that everything was fine and that the nice fairy was going to take her back to the village. I shall never forget the look of fear that I saw that day on Kaznia's face.

She told me to tell her where the princess was, then to find King Peteron and tell him to come quickly. Her voice was panic stricken. We rushed to find King Peteron. By the time we returned to where the princess was, Queen Kaznia was lying fatally wounded; a twisted ugly creature was standing over her, laughing. Blood was dripping from its' teeth, its' eyes were a piercing yellow." "What about the princess?" "Michelalena was lying on the ground peacefully as though she were asleep. King Peteron almost died himself, fighting off the evil Dragonscott, but he is a strong leader. Thankfully, he badly wounded Dragonscott, who fled back to his underground lair. Peteron carried his beloved queen back to his village. I carried the tiny princess in my hand. Within moments of reaching the village she woke, having no idea what had happened.

Sadly, it was not the same for the queen; even with the most powerful fairy magic she could not be saved. Peteron almost died of a broken heart. It was a long time after that before any of our fairy friends visited us. I felt responsible for what had happened until Nanamic the Wise visited me one early morning. She explained to me that the Bawllows are cunning and devious and that they have the ability to trick fairies, so it was only to be expected that they could trick humans, especially an eleven year old girl.

Anyway that was my first encounter with a Bawllow. I wish I could say it was also my last but alas, I have encountered them several times since. One thing is for sure, you must never underestimate them, to do so could be devastating. Dragonscott is by far the worst, but there are others who are equally horrible." "Have you seen them?" "One or two. Jeanadag is the most wicked. They say she enjoys torturing gnomes because they don't have the power to fight her off. The gnomes and the fairies may have their differences but one thing is certain, they both have a fear, along with hatred for the Bawllows.

Stories are told amongst the fairies that the entrance to the Bawllows' lair is marked with the tortured corpses of gnomes." "Are the stories true, Aunt Clara?" "I really cannot say, never having seen it. There is one Bawllow who they say still has some good in her." "Who is she?" "Her name is Selandria. According to Princess Bellaruth and Prince Iandrew, King Peteron's other children, Selandria was once a very beautiful fairy. Bellaruth and Selandria used to play together when they were small, but then one day, she simply disappeared. They searched and searched for her; they feared that she had been kidnapped or killed. But no trace was ever found until years later when a fairy baby was taken. The child's parents told Nanamic that a fairy fitting Selandria's description had helped them rescue the child from the Bawllows' lair. Nanamic believes that she was enchanted by Dragonscott and was so mesmerised by him that he controls her, although she retained some of her fairy goodness. In case either of you should ever run into her, be warned that she can shape shift into any animal; her particular favourite being that of a beautiful white horse and be in no doubt that she will harm you if Dragonscott demands it.

Well that's about it, do you to understand now?" asked Clara. "We think so," came the reply. "When are you going to teach us how to do magic?" said Jamie excitedly. "Perhaps I will start tomorrow, there is much for you to learn, not just magic. I will need to teach you about herbs for healing and herbs to help ward off evil. Sometimes, the simplest thing, like a particular plant or root could save a life and you must always remember that these gifts that you have inherited are not just there for helping fairies. In time you will find that you can help many people and animals. There are also people who can help you.

Take Tom, for instance. He's no ordinary farmer, quite the opposite in fact." "Is Tom like us, does he have the birthmark?" "No my dears, but he is a good man and Nanamic saw fit to bestow Tom with certain gifts, for instance, the ability to see them when others cannot." "Why did they choose Tom, Aunt Clara?" "Well many years ago, the woodland behind Tom's farm was going to be sold, which would have been terrible for the fairy folk that live there; so I asked Tom not to sell it and like a true friend he didn't. He never questioned as to why, so Nanamic agreed that through such a selfless act he should at least have an explanation. I suppose the fairies see him as a sort of guardian; even when Tom dies, the land will never be sold." "How?" "Simple; because Tom has no family he's left it to me and I've left it to you and no doubt you will pass it on to your children and so on. So you see, Tom is a good man who you could always go to if you were in trouble. In fact, I think that's where we'll go today. I know Tom is keen for you two to see his new litter of piglets and I promised him some jam, so you run along and get ready and then we'll set off." "Oh Aunt Clara, can't you tell us some more about the fairies?" "There's plenty of time for you to learn and it's a lovely day outside. It would be a shame to waste it, God only knows the winter comes soon enough in England, so come on let's be having you."

CHAPTER FIVE
Remedies

"Gosh! Is it much further to Tom's house?" puffed Jamie. "Oh not too far now; actually, this stretch of woodland is where several fairy folk dwell, so mind you two stick to the path, we don't want to go treading on something we shouldn't. Our tiny friends wouldn't like that now would they?" "What, you mean like their houses Aunt Clara?" "No my dear Maddy, their houses would never be this close to the footpath. I mean some of the plants; they're what are used to make fairy medicine, along with other ingredients." "Are those the herbs and things you were talking about earlier?" enquired Maddy. "Yes my dear, the very same. In fact, on our way back we'll pick some so I can teach you what each one is for." "That would be great," said Maddy." "I have a feeling my dear, that you will be the healer like me and Jamie will take after Sally and take to the magic side of things." Jamie's ears pricked up. "Are we going to learn some magic today Aunt Clara?" "We'll see my boy." Clara noticed a look of disappointment on her nephew's face. "I expect we'll have time for a little magic, perhaps this evening." "WICKED!" exclaimed Jamie. Clara and Maddy laughed. "Ah there's Tom's house," said Clara.

The twins where quite surprised to see how rundown it was. The barns looked as though they would collapse at any moment, especially if there was a strong wind. The gate, which gave access to the adjoining field, was broken and half of it was lying in the mud. There where old cans littering the yard and a rusty old tractor, which looked as if it had probably not been used for twenty

33

years. Jamie muttered to Maddy under his breath that Tom lived in a salvage yard (the English equivalent being a scrap yard.) "Now that's not very nice Jamie," said Clara, having heard him. "This is a big farm for Tom to run and he doesn't have anyone to help him, so certain things get left, but he looks after his pigs really well. He's a good kind man, so let's not say nasty things about him."

Jamie felt rather humbled by Aunt Clara. To try and make up for it, he told Clara that if Tom wanted, he would help him tidy things up a bit. Clara grinned. "I'm sure Tom would like that; in fact perhaps that's just what he needs to motivate him. I'll mention it to him; maybe we could all give him a hand?" "I don't mind," said Maddy. "Ah there's Tom," said Clara, as she waved out to him. "'Ello," called Tom "tiz is a nice surprise, I didn't 'spect you till the end of the week." "Well I had a batch of jams made so we thought we would walk over with them" said Clara, "Tiz very kind of ya, I'll be 'aving some of that for me supper, but in the meantime can I be gittin you good people something to drink? No doubt that walk has tuckered ya all out." "Thank you Tom," said Clara. "I'm sure a nice cold glass of lemon would go down a treat." "Then consider it done, three glasses of lemon comin' up."

Clara and the twins followed Tom into his farmhouse. The twins couldn't help giggling when Tom threw a chicken out the door. It had been sitting on the sink drainer. "Damn' chickens," said Tom "they got a perfickly good henhouse but fa some reason they seem to prefer it'n me kitchen." Just by looking round the kitchen, the twins could tell that no-one helped Tom with the housework. There was washing up piled into the sink, a stack of old newspapers covered the table; nothing appeared to be put in its rightful place. "Shall we take our drinks outside?" suggested Clara. "Good idea!" said Tom looking a bit embarrassed by the mess in his kitchen. "Anyways I've got something to show the twins, follow me."

Tom led them across the yard to a large barn. Lying in a large pile of straw, the twins could see a huge pig. At least ten piglets were suckling from her. "Oh they're lovely," said Maddy, edging a little closer to them. She noticed that one piglet was much smaller than the others and it appeared to have been pushed out by them. "Why is that one so small Tom?" she asked. "Ah tha'll be the runt, don't think tha' little fella is gonna make it." "Oh why?" asked Maddy. "Can't git 'im to feed, I think 'e's too weak ta suck." "Isn't there something you can do Tom?" "I've tried jus' about everythin' I know, 'e's just too small. If I could just git 'im ta drink from the bottle, 'e may stand a chance." "Can I try?" asked Maddy. "Course ya can, sit yaself down on that stool an' I'll pass him to ya."

Tom handed over the tiny piglet followed by a baby's feeding bottle full of milk. Maddy gently placed the teat to its mouth. At first, the tiny piglet didn't seem at all interested, he was so weak, but Maddy tried to encourage it by dripping the milk onto her finger then dripping tiny droplets into its mouth. Within minutes it was sucking from the bottle. It hardly stopped to take in air. "Well I'll be blessed!" exclaimed Tom. "I thought the little fella was gonna die; she 'as a way with animals that niece of yours Clara." "I don't doubt it Tom, I've been telling them about things." "Oh 'ave ya now Clara, so they know about our little magical friends then?" "Yes Tom. I thought it was time to let them know who they are." "'Spose you're right Clara you know best, prob'ly just as well." "What makes you say that Tom?" "Well I'll tell ya Clara, there's somethin' goin' on." "Going on Tom?" "Oh yes Clara! For the past few nights I've been 'earing things." "Things Tom? What sort of things?" "Noises comin' from the woods, lots of lights dartin' about, whisperin' voices, that sorta thing. I tell ya Clara, somethin's afoot." "Well no doubt we'll hear about it soon enough Tom." "Can I hold a piglet?" asked Jamie. "Course ya can," said Tom, "Well, we best be getting off home soon," said Clara. "Would you care to join us for lunch Tom?" "I won't thank ye Clara. I've got loads to do, per'aps another time eh." "My door is always open Tom, you know that." "I do Clara." "Come on you two, put those piglets back, we best be getting off home." "Oh just a couple more minutes?" begged Maddy "He's nearly drunk the whole bottle," referring to the piglet. "Just two more minutes," said Clara. Maddy asked Tom if he thought the little piglet would survive. She was pleased to hear that he thought it would, now that it had started to feed. As the three of them made their way back to the cottage, Clara kept stopping to pick plants. She laid them carefully in a basket that she had taken with her to carry Tom's jam in. By the time they reached the cottage the basket was full. "I expect you two are hungry?" said Clara. "Starving!" replied Jamie. "Then I suggest we have lunch before I tell you two about these plants." The twins both nodded their heads in agreement.

CHAPTER SIX

Beginner's Magic

"Have you two had enough to eat? enquired Clara. "Yes thank you." "Then might I suggest we get on with your first lesson." "Are we going to do some magic? asked Jamie. "Oh I expect so, but first I want you to learn about the plants I've picked today, while they're still fresh. No good trying to show you once they've withered." Aunt Clara began by showing them how to grind some of the plants. She had a small bowl with a wooden tool that had a rounded knob on the end. The twins watched as Clara placed a few leaves from some of the plants into the bowl, then using the wooden grinder, she mashed them all together. Jamie grimaced as Clara offered him the bowl to smell. "Agh, It's horrible Aunt Clara, it smells disgusting and it doesn't look any better either!" he exclaimed.

Clara passed the bowl to Maddy. She agreed with Jamie. "Pass me those tiny jars Maddy, the ones on the dresser behind you." Maddy passed Clara a tray with lots of tiny jars and bottles on. Some of the labels looked familiar to her. There was essence of lavender, vanilla, sandalwood, lemon grass, witch hazel, and a jar of thick brown honey, to mention but a few. Maddy had seen her mother use these things if ever the twins had hurt themselves. Sally would rub witch hazel on their skin if they had a bad bruise; for upset tummies Sally would add certain liquids to warm milk. Maddy had never given it any thought before, but thinking about it now, she couldn't ever remember going to see a doctor, other than Sally, neither her nor Jamie. "Ok you two," said Clara, "now listen carefully. The plants I have ground are very good in bringing down a fever if you add a little lemon grass to them." "What! Would someone have to eat them?" asked Jamie with a horrified look on his face. "Good heavens no, my dear boy! You would place the mixture in a cloth and lay it on them. If they had an open wound you would place the cloth directly over the wound. I've shown you this one first, simply because it's the one I use most often. More importantly, can you two remember which plants I used?" "I think I can," said Maddy. "Show me." Maddy looked through the remaining plants in Clara's basket and selected four different ones. "Well done Maddy," said Clara. "I'll tell you all the names of the plants at a later time, no good trying to learn too much to start with. What about you Jamie, would you have known which plants?" "I think so Aunt Clara."

For the next three hours, Clara showed the twins every combination of remedies. She could sense that Jamie was finding the whole thing slightly boring. "Well I think that's enough for one afternoon, shall we have a nice fresh cup of tea? Then afterwards perhaps we'll try a little magic." Suddenly Jamie seemed to come to life. "That would be great!" He could barely contain his excitement. "Magic it is then." said Clara. "I'll make the tea while you two find me a few things. Jamie, run outside and fetch me some flowers from the garden, only a few mind, about a dozen should do it. Maddy, you look in the cupboard under the sink and find me a flower vase."

Within minutes the twins were back at the table with their items. Clara poured them all a cup of tea. Jamie began to fidget. "Patience my boy, patience," said Clara. "They finished their tea and Aunt Clara cleared away the tray. On her return to the table, she took some pieces of fruit from a bowl on the dresser. Placing them in front of her on the table, she mumbled to herself, "that should do it." The twins sat quietly waiting for the magic to begin. "Right then," said Clara, "shall we begin?" The twins nodded in approval. "Then watch and listen," said Clara.

Placing an apple in the centre of the table, she pointed her finger at it and clearly spoke some magic words. The twins watched in amazement as Clara said "LEVITUS, LEVITUS." Slowly the apple began to rise from the table, only stopping when Clara told it to. The twins could not believe their eyes. Clara watched as it hovered in the air about two feet above them, she did the same thing with a pear and two plums. Pointing her finger at the fruit again she spoke the words "DESENDIUS, DESENDIUS." Slowly the fruit moved down towards the table. Everything was going to plan until the fruit was about four inches from the table top, when suddenly they dropped like stones, hitting the surface and rolling onto the floor, all except for the pear, which Jamie managed to catch. "OH bother!" sighed Clara. "I can never quite get it right, that always happens!" "Aunt Clara, that was fantastic!" stated Jamie. "Can I try now?" "Very well," said Clara. "Do you remember the magic words?" "Yes." "Ok then, you try Jamie, but remember to concentrate."

Jamie took a deep breath, then pointing at the apple, "LEVITUS, LEVITUS." Immediately the apple began to rise. Jamie soon had the other pieces of fruit in the air. "Don't break concentration," said Clara, "but now bring them down." Jamie didn't flinch as he said "DESENDIUS, DESENDIUS." Slowly, all four pieces made their way down to the table, only unlike Clara's, they gently landed on the table in a neat group. "How was that?" said Jamie, looking rather proud of himself. "Very good my boy, very good indeed. You are obviously a natural," said Clara. "It was dead easy," boasted Jamie. Clara smiled over at Maddy. "Let's see if you are as talented as your brother."

Maddy calmly pointed at the fruit; she spoke the magic words, anyone watching her would never have guessed it was her first attempt at magic; she was so composed, unlike Jamie, who was already fidgeting, waiting for another go. "Very well done Maddy," said Aunt Clara. "Now I want you both to try something else, something a little more difficult." She instructed the twins to go and stand at opposite ends of the kitchen. Once she was satisfied there was enough distance between them, she explained that she wanted them to send a piece of fruit across the room to each other. "How do we do it? asked Maddy, "We only know how to make it go up and down." "Good point," replied Clara, "although it's really quite simple. You just tell the fruit where you want it to go. You only need the magic words to start the spell. Let's start with you Jamie,"

Clara tossed an apple towards him. He caught it deftly and laid it in the palm of his hand, then, using the magic words, the apple slowly rose upwards only a few inches when he told it to stop. Pointing at Maddy, he directed the apple towards her. When the apple was a few inches away from her, he left it hovering in the air. Maddy stretched out her arm, turning her hand palm up. Jamie spoke the magic words and slowly and gently the apple came to rest in the palm of his sister's hand. "Bravo! Bravo!" said Clara with a gentle clap of her hands. "Well done Jamie, I see that you two are going to pick things up very quickly." Clara had no doubt that Maddy would do as well as her brother and of course, she was right. Maddy sailed through the exercise. "Perhaps we'll try something a little more difficult," said Clara as she placed the flower vase in the centre of the table. "Where are the flowers you picked earlier Jamie?" "I left them on the drainer, shall I bring them over?" Clara smiled. "No need, we'll do it with magic."

Clara told the twins to stay at opposite ends of the room, then using the magic, they were to move the flowers one by one and place them in the vase on the table, the vase only having a small neck. "No problem," boasted Jamie, "just sit back and enjoy the show." Clara and Maddy chuckled. One by one the twins took turns at moving a flower from the drainer to the vase. It was only when they had achieved this several times that they realised how difficult it was becoming. Jamie's last attempt ended in a broken stem and the flower lying next to the vase on the table. Maddy did manage one more than her brother before falling to the same problem. Clara watched as the twins became more and more frustrated. Jamie was becoming quite agitated with the whole process. Finally the twins admitted defeat; they simply could not make all the flowers fit into the vase. "Come and sit down," said Clara. Once seated, Clara asked them what they had learnt from the exercise. Jamie was, as always, the first to answer. "Yes Jamie, what have you gained from that?" asked Clara. Looking rather smug, Jamie replied, "Next time, when arranging flowers, use a bigger vase!" Clara could not hold back a tiny chuckle before answering. "What if you didn't have a bigger vase?" Jamie tried to think of an answer. Clara asked Maddy what she thought. Thinking it over, Maddy said that perhaps even with magic, there where some things that simply could not be done. "Exactly my dear!" exclaimed Clara. "There are some things that cannot be done, even with the help of magic. I knew that the vase would only hold five or six stems, yet you two tried to put double that amount in. Do you see the point I'm trying to make?" The twins nodded. "Good, then your first lesson has been a success, so might I suggest that whilst I'm preparing the vegetables for tea, you two run along and practise some basic magic. I'll call you when tea is ready."

The twins could not wait to try some more magic. They hurriedly left the table. Clara watched the twins as she peeled the vegetables for the evening meal. She was actually quite impressed with the young pair. She chuckled quietly to herself as Jamie tried to outdo Maddy by moving larger objects, and spinning them round in the air, but the young apprentice Maddy was having none of it, her motto being, if he can do it so can I. There was no doubt in Clara's mind that it would not be long before the twins were both relatively accomplished witches.

CHAPTER SEVEN

Secrets

After tea, Clara showed the twins more potions. She noticed that Maddy seemed to take great pleasure in blending just the right ingredients; her natural qualities as a healer shone through. It was obvious, however, that Jamie definitely preferred magic. Clara explained to the twins that they must never discuss their gifts with anyone outside of the watcher's circle, only ever with people who could be totally trusted. Jamie seemed a little disappointed. He had hoped to be able to impress his friends back in the States with his new found powers, although he understood why secrecy would be of the utmost importance.

Every day the twins were taught something new by Aunt Clara. It was such an exciting time for them. Even the times when Clara had to remind them to phone their parents seemed to be an inconvenience to Maddy and Jamie. Not that they didn't love Sally and John, they did. It's just that it meant a drive into the village to use the phone, which seemed to take forever to connect to the States, then only speaking to Sally and John for a few minutes. Many times when they rang, Sally and

John would be asleep and the phone would ring for ages before they answered. Jamie had readily told Sally about Aunt Clara teaching them everything. She told him to listen carefully to what Clara said and that he should wait until they returned home to talk about it, as you never know who might be listening.

Time seemed to fly by; the twins learnt something new every day. Tom had also become an important part of their teachings. Like Clara, he was very knowledgeable about fairy ways and all the different plants and flowers used for all types of things. Aunt Clara also devised a plan, so that they could help Tom clean up his house. She used the excuse that it would be a good lesson for the twins if they could practice their magic skills to put things away in a neat and tidy fashion, although they did have to help repair the gate and barn without the aid of magic. It was too risky out in the open in case someone should see them.

Maddy looked forward to going to Tom's. The tiny piglet, which she had fed two weeks earlier, was now thriving and growing bigger by the day. It followed Maddy all around Tom's farm. He had named it Apple, sort of a reminder of the States, where Maddy came from; (New York - the Big Apple.) Tom promised Maddy that Apple would never be sold at market for meat; instead he would be kept as a pet.

CHAPTER EIGHT
Meeting Wickit

Clara told the twins that they were to expect a visitor. "Who?" enquired Jamie. "Wickit!" "Yippee! We're finally going to meet a real fairy!" he shouted. "Will we meet him today?" asked Maddy "and will it be just him?" "I think so," replied Clara, "Tom saw him a couple of evenings ago. Apparently, our little friends are very keen to meet you. I'm surprised one of them hasn't been round sooner, but Tom tells me that things don't seem quite right amongst the fairy folk." "What do you mean, not quite right?" asked Jamie. "No doubt we'll find out soon enough," said Clara. "What time will he come?" enquired Maddy." "Oh, usually around eight o'clock or thereabouts, he has a terrible habit of startling folk. I remember one particular evening, I was sitting quietly in the armchair doing my knitting, when all of a sudden, Wickit shot out of the fireplace. He had fallen down the chimney; his little wings were quite badly singed!" Clara let out a tiny chuckle. "Was he ok?" asked Maddy, looking quite concerned. "Oh yes my dear, he was fine but it served him right for trying to startle me." "Yep, that's Wickit!" laughed Jamie.

"How do you to fancy a game of snakes and ladders after tea tonight?" "Aunt Clara, we haven't played that game for years," joked Maddy. "Neither have I," replied Clara, "so how about it then?" "Ok!" came the joint reply. Jamie could not wait for the evening to arrive so he could meet Wickit. Teatime could not come quickly enough; they always ate around five o'clock and he knew that by the time they had eaten, it would not be that long before Wickit's visit.

Finally, the words he had been waiting for. "Tea's ready!" "What's that lovely smell?" asked Maddy, as she came in from outside. "Ah, that will be my home-made rabbit stew," boasted Clara. "Rabbit," stated a rather wide eyed Maddy, "we don't have rabbit back home!" "I know," said Clara, "that's why I always cook it for Sally when she's over here." "What! Mum likes it?" "Oh yes my dear and if my memory serves me correctly, so do you and your brother." "Aunt Clara, I'm sure we've never eaten it," said a rather put out Maddy. "Well my dear, I'm sure you have. It's just that until today you didn't know what it was. Most people think they're eating chicken."

The twins looked at the meal in front of them. As always, it looked delicious, with a selection of freshly grown vegetables accompanying the casserole, but the thought of eating a rabbit did little to encourage their appetites. "Tuck in," said Clara, "how do you know whether or not you like it, if you don't taste it? It's really no different from eating pork, chicken, lamb or any other kind of meat for that matter." Gingerly, Jamie stabbed his fork into the meat, slowly raising it to his mouth. "Here goes," he said, looking at Maddy. She watched as he placed the fork in his mouth. "It's delicious!" he exclaimed, quickly filling his fork with the next mouthful. Maddy decided to try it. "You're right Jamie, it really is nice." Aunt Clara held back a chuckle. "If there's any left, we'll invite Tom for lunch tomorrow; I know it's his favourite." The twins were too busy eating to answer her. Their bellies where soon full and their plates empty.

As Clara and Maddy cleared the dishes from the table, ready for washing, Clara suggested that Jamie set about clearing the table, ready for their game of snakes and ladders. "There now, that didn't take us long did it? Jamie sort the game out, you'll find the box with the snakes and ladders in over in the top drawer of the dresser." "Hurriedly, Jamie placed the tatty old box on the table. "Gosh!" said Maddy, "that's what you call a relic." It was the most basic snakes and ladders board, no fancy designs or colours, together with four tiny different coloured discs made of plastic, which over the years had worn away quite considerably and a small plastic cup in which to shake the dice. "Well," said Clara, "someone bought me that for my sixth birthday." "Your sixth! gasped Jamie, "God that's so old!" "Careful!" said Clara, peering at Jamie over her specs, with a raised eyebrow. "Oh ARGH, UMM, what I meant was that it's in really good condition considering how (Jamie paused for a moment, not wishing to imply again that Aunt Clara was old) many times it must have been used over the years." Clara smiled at Jamie. "Tactfully put, my dear boy. For a moment there, I thought you were going to tell me how old I am getting!" "OH NO, Aunt Clara, you're not old," stated Jamie, trying hard to redeem himself. Suddenly Clara burst into laughter. "Oh my dear Jamie if you could only see yourself! I'm just toying with you; I know I'm getting old. My poor old bones tell me every morning, especially when the weather is damp."

The three of them were still laughing whilst picking which colour they wanted to be in the game. "Can I be red?" asked Maddy. "Of course my dear." "I'll be blue," said Jamie. "Then I shall be green," said Clara. "Do we have to throw a six or something to see who goes first?" enquired Maddy. "No my dear, what we do is, everyone has a throw and whoever throws the highest number starts the game. Once the game is started, if you throw a six you get an extra go." "Oh that's right," said Maddy, "I knew it was something like that."

They each took their turn. Jamie threw a four as did Clara, but Maddy threw a six first time, so she began the game. Aunt Clara appeared to be thoroughly enjoying herself. She hadn't played a game for at least two years; the last time being when Tom had stayed for tea. Jamie glanced over at the clock. He was shocked to see that it was already a quarter past seven. The time since tea had passed much quicker than he thought it would. "Do you think Wickit will definitely come tonight Aunt Clara?" "Oh I'm sure he will my dear, in fact he should be along any time now." Maddy interrupted. "Come on Jamie it's your go!" she snapped. Patience was normally her strong point, but in fact every time she seemed to be winning, she would find herself sliding down a snake and she had really lost heart, wanting the game to end. "OK misery, just because you're losing and I'm winning!" said Jamie, as he shook the dice and rolled a five. He moved his counter along five spaces and informed his sister that he only needed three to win the game. "Looks like I'll need nothing short of a miracle for me to win," chuckled Clara, noticing that her green counter was at least twenty spaces behind Jamie's. Shaking the dice vigorously, Clara threw a six. Maddy offered to move her counter for her. "You get another go" said Jamie, "for throwing a six." "Oh so I do my boy, it's so long since I've thrown a six I had forgotten you get an extra go." "Another six!" cheered Maddy. "Throw again Aunt Clara. Another six, that's three six's in a row!" she exclaimed! "Throw again, yippee! Another six, this is fantastic!" beamed Maddy. "One more six and you'll be on the same line as Jamie, just eight spaces behind him in fact." Clara shook the dice again. "Yippee!" shouted Maddy, "another six, you only need a five now to win." Aunt Clara didn't look very impressed with her sudden run of luck. "Throw the dice Aunt Clara!" The trio watched as the dice rolled across the table, appearing to stop at number two, only then to suddenly flip over twice to the number five. "Well done Aunt Clara, you won!" shrilled an excited Maddy. "What a comeback," said Jamie, in a rather deflated voice, "but well done Aunt Clara."

The twins were surprised by what Aunt Clara said next. She simply crossed her arms, sat back in her chair and said in a very clear voice, "Ok, you can come out now." The twins looked baffled. Who was Aunt Clara talking to? Clara repeated herself, only this time adding, "don't be shy now, come on." Suddenly they noticed a tiny light glowing from behind one of the pots on the dresser. "Come on Wickit, come and say hello to Jamie and Maddy," said Clara, "they're eager to meet you." The twins watched, their eyes wide, their mouths open as a tiny figure stepped out from behind the jar. Suddenly, without warning, Wickit leapt from the dresser to the table.

There he stood right in front of them, eyeing them up and down, his hands on his hips, feet apart. Maddy was quite mesmerized by Wickit's beautiful vivid blue eyes and his pointed ears; his fine golden hair which hung down his tunic from being tucked behind his ears. However, by far the most fascinating things were Wickit's tiny wings. They were almost transparent, so delicate, and finer than even the most delicate butterfly wings. Maddy noticed that each time Wickit moved his wings, tiny particles of silver dust seem to cascade from them. Stepping forward to introduce himself, "you must be Maddy?" he said, as he bent forward and rolled his hand over in the air so as to bow like a nobleman, repeating the performance to Jamie. "Your Aunt Clara has told me all about you both and I've been keeping an eye on you over these past years. I must say I was pretty impressed with the magic and stuff; you kids certainly pick things up quickly. I hope we'll be seeing a lot of each other; perhaps I will be able to teach you some things." "That's very kind of you Wickit," said Clara. "Not at all, it's the least I can do, especially with me being Jamie's favourite and all," he laughed, sneaking a look at Jamie who blushed furiously. "Although I have to agree with the fair Maddy, the Princess Melissa is indeed a rare prize."

Clara and the twins noticed that no sooner had Wickit mentioned the name Melissa, than he seemed to go off into a sort of a daydream; in fact Wickit himself was not even aware that whilst in a daydream, he was actually floating slowly towards the ceiling. It was only when Aunt Clara coughed that he snapped out of it.

"Anyway Wickit, how are King Peteron and his family?" asked Clara. "They are well, thank you Clara. They send you their best wishes from all in the village. The King wishes you to bring the twins along to the village to meet everyone." "Fantastic!" said Jamie, his sister nodding in agreement. "King Peteron apologises for not inviting you all sooner, but all has not been well in the village. "Nothing serious, I hope? said Clara." "Oh I'm sure it will pass; anyway Nanamic the Wise will no doubt explain everything to you. She's very much looking forward to seeing you Clara; she loves her chats with you. Sadly, now I must be going. Come to the clearing in the woods tomorrow at half past seven but wait for my signal Clara. Be extra vigilant, there's things going on in the woods. I'll be looking out for you, see you tomorrow." With that, there was a flash of light and Wickit was gone. A moment passed. Aunt Clara was just about to speak to the twins when suddenly, there was another flash of light and standing back in front of them was Wickit. "Sorry, almost forgot, King Peteron sends his congratulations to the twins for being such good apprentices. It has not gone unnoticed, how hard you have both been trying. That's all! Bye again!" Another flash and Wickit had gone again.

Aunt Clara shook her head and raised her eyebrows. "Well, that was the famous Wickit." "Oh! He was so beautiful," said Maddy, "but so tiny." "I can't wait till tomorrow," said Jamie, excitedly, "we're going to a real fairy village." Aunt Clara pushed her glasses along her nose; somehow this made her look rather sterner. "Yes," she stated, "you two will need to be on your very best behaviour, it's a very great honour to be invited to a fairy village."

CHAPTER NINE

Magic at the Farm

Winston gave his early morning alarm call. The twins were eager to get up, this was the day they would be visiting the fairy village. "Breakfast is ready," called Clara. As they ate their breakfast, all they could think about was the visit. Jamie asked Clara what time they would need to leave to get to the meeting place. "Oh, about seven o'clock." Jamie looked disappointed, that seemed so long to wait. "I have a busy day planned for us," said Clara. "Seven o' clock will be here before you know it." Jamie smiled. "What are we doing today?" asked Maddy. "Well, I thought we could visit Tom and perhaps help him tidy up a bit around the farm." "Great," said Maddy, maybe I can feed Apple again." "Oh I'm sure you will my dear," replied Clara. "Have you two had enough to eat?" "Sure have, we're stuffed, that was delicious," said Jamie. "Well in that case, might I suggest that you two run along and get ready, so we can set off for Tom's?"

Within fifteen minutes the twins were ready to go. Jamie seemed to make less fuss about the distance between Clara's and Tom's. He was actually beginning to enjoy the country walks. The twins told Clara about things they do back in the States. According to Maddy, her brother was quite an accomplished skateboarder, having won several trophies. Maddy was very talented at gymnastics and art. She had won a gold medal for gymnastics along with several silvers and a bronze. Clara was impressed with the way John and Sally had brought the twins up; especially when she knew about the terrible drug problems they have with youngsters in the States and how so many children get in with the wrong crowd. Street gangs were a big worry to parents in America. Yes, in all, Clara was very happy with her two young wards.

"There's Tom," said Maddy, as she waved out to him. "'Ello there," called Tom, "'tis a nice surprise, I weren't 'spectin' comp'nee." "How's Apple?" asked Maddy. "Oh 'e's doin' just fine. In fact, I'm sure 'e'll probably be one of the most intelligent pigs I've ever 'ad; unlike the others, 'e seems to know 'is name, some days 'e even follows me roun' like a dog." Clara and the twins couldn't stop laughing. Tom even afforded himself a chuckle. "Oh Tom, that's so funny," said Clara, "a porker called Apple, who thinks he's a dog." "I think it's great!" piped Maddy. "Why don't you kids go an' check 'im out? Ya know where 'e is." No sooner had he asked and the twins were heading off towards the barn.

Clara and Tom walked towards the farmhouse. "I hope you don't mind us visiting? It's just that I know Jamie cannot wait 'til tonight, so we needed to kill some time," explained Clara. "Not at all," said Tom, "I likes it when ya come over. 'Tis nice to 'ave compnee, but wat's goin' on tonight, if ya don't mind me askin'?" "Of course not Tom, it's just that this evening we have been invited to the village. Young Jamie is so excited, so you see why I needed to occupy him; which brings me to asking you a favour." "Anythin' Clara, ya know I'll always 'elp if I can." "Well Tom, I thought it would be a good idea if the twins could show you the magic they have learnt; Jamie is a natural born show off and it will pass the time." "Wot a good idea Clara, wot do ya 'ave in mind?" "Well perhaps we could let them tidy the house for you using only magic. I've let them wash up and pack things away for me. They're really quite good and perhaps Jamie could help you mend a few things around the farm, that broken gate for instance?" "Sounds good ta me Clara, but do ya think they're gonna wanna do it?" "Oh for sure Tom, for sure." "Best go and find 'em then Clara."

Tom and Clara made their way to the barn. As they approached, they could hear Maddy talking to Apple. It was obvious that there was a definite bond between them. As Clara and Tom entered the barn, Maddy called to them to watch. She walked to the far side of the barn and began to call Apple. They watched, as without hesitation, the tiny piglet left its' mother and hurried across to Maddy, who was only too keen to pick him up and give him a cuddle. "Well I'll be blessed," said Tom. "I ain't ever seen a pig so tame. I reckons he does think 'e's a dog!" They all laughed. "The little fella must be gittin' 'ungry, do ya wanna feed 'im Maddy?" "Oh yes please!" Tom handed her a bottle of milk he had made earlier."Gosh!" said Maddy, "now I know why they call pigs porkers," as the tiny piglet almost pulled the bottle from her hand in his eagerness to eat.

"How do you two fancy showing Tom how good you've become at magic?" Aunt Clara asked the twins. "Sure, what would you like us to do?" enquired an ever confident Jamie. "Well I thought we could start in the house with some basic cleaning and tidying." "Ugh! You mean housework," sighed Jamie. "Not just housework," replied Clara. "I thought you could help Tom mend some things around the farm, maybe you could even see if you could get that old tractor to go." "Yeah that would be great," said Jamie. "But I think we'll start in the house first," said Clara, "so when you two are finished with Apple, come over to the house. We'll go and put the kettle on, ready for a cuppa." "Sounds good ta me," beamed Tom.

Back in the barn, Jamie was moaning to his sister about housework being woman's work and that she and Clara should do the house while he and Tom worked in the yard. "Don't be such a chauvinist!" said Maddy. "Anyway, you know why Aunt Clara is doing it?" "Why?" "It's because Aunt Clara doesn't want to embarrass Tom. This is her way of helping him and at the same time, letting Tom think he's helping her, stupid." "I knew that," quipped Jamie." "Of course you did," said Maddy in a sarcastic tone, knowing that Jamie didn't have a clue about Aunt Clara's intentions. "Good timin'," said Tom, as the twins entered the house. "Yer Aunt Clara's just about to pour the tea, unless you kids would prefer a glass of lemon?" They both nodded their heads in approval of lemon.

"Would you two like to get started?" "Yes!" "Tom and I will just sit back and watch, or as Jamie would put it, sit back and enjoy the show!" They all chuckled. Maddy told Jamie that the sink would probably be as good a place to start as any and he agreed. Maddy pointed her finger at the taps and spoke the magic words 'LEVITUS LEVITUS'. Within seconds the sink was filling with water. Jamie ordered the washing up liquid into the running water and within a few minutes, the sink was cleared of all Tom's dirty dishes. "I'm impressed!" said Tom. Clara and Tom watched as the broom swept the floor, a cloth wiped down all the work surfaces and crockery and cutlery was put away in cupboards. Within minutes the kitchen looked spick and span. "How was that?" boasted Jamie. "Very impressive," said Tom, "I can't ever remember when me kitchin looked sa nice." "May I make a suggestion?" asked Clara. The trio nodded. "So as we don't get under each others feet, what about Tom and Jamie working outside, while Maddy and I finish in the house?" "Great idea Aunt Clara," said Jamie. "Is that all right with you Tom?" "Well, seein' as young Jamie is sa keen I s'pose I best agree." Clara smiled at Tom. "That's settled then, we'll see you two later." Jamie was already out the door, calling to Tom that he would meet him by the old tractor.

"Will you be doing magic with me Aunt Clara?" asked Maddy. "Of course my dear," replied Aunt Clara, "believe me, I need the practice." Maddy couldn't help laughing to herself as she watched Aunt Clara. No doubt about it, Aunt Clara was definitely out of practice. She misjudged so many things, like the drawers on Tom's sideboard. If she wanted the top drawer to open, so as to put something away, the bottom one would open. Even Clara saw the funny side of it. "I think I should stick to remedies," she chuckled to Maddy. "Nonsense," said Maddy, "it's only because you don't use magic all the time." "Maybe you're right my dear. Truth is, I've never really been that keen, not like you and Jamie. It comes naturally to you, as it did your mother."

Even with Clara's mistakes, it was not long before the house was like a new pin. "I hope Tom will be pleased," said Maddy. "Oh I'm sure he will be," replied Clara, "but I think before we go and find Tom and your brother, I'll make us a nice cup of tea. I'd forgotten just how tiring magic can be." "You sit down Aunt Clara, I'll make the tea." "Thank you Maddy, that would be lovely. Remember to top the pot up in case the others want one.

Outside in the yard things were also going well. Tom and Jamie had managed to get the old tractor going, although only for a few minutes at a time. The gate was repaired and tiles were back on the house roof. "This looks good," said a voice they both recognised as Clara's. "It does indeed," said Tom, "fact is, I can't remember when t'old place looked so good." "Would you care for a nice cup of tea," asked Clara, "we've just made a pot." "That'll be grand," replied Tom. As the four of them sat around the table drinking their tea, Clara noticed that Tom kept looking round the kitchen; a slight sadness seemed to hang over him. "Is everything alright Tom? asked Clara. "'Tis better than alright Clara, I can't believe it's me old 'ouse lookin' sa fine. I can't thank ye all enough." "Nonsense Tom, it should be us who should be thanking you." "How's so?" "Well Tom you let us take up your time, allow the twins to practice their magic, and more to the point, almost four hours have passed, so we had better be thinking about heading home for some lunch. We would very much like you to join us; it's been too long since you came over for lunch." "Oh go on Tom," pleaded Maddy. "There's nothing for you to do here, everything's done and you know what a wonderful cook Aunt Clara is." "Ah that I do, ya would 'a made someone a good wife Clara, that's fa sure." "Oh get away with you Tom," said Clara, blushing the colour of beetroot. The twins glanced across at each other, both thinking that Tom definitely had a soft spot for Aunt Clara. "Go on Tom," said Jamie. "I'll tell ya wot, if you two 'elps me feed me pigs, I'll come fa lunch." "Deal," said Jamie. Maddy agreed.

CHAPTER TEN

Tom Comes for Lunch

Back at Clara's, Tom chatted to the twins while Clara prepared lunch. "Somethin' smells good," said Tom. "Aunt Clara made a rabbit stew yesterday, there was some left over for today," said Maddy. "Yep, I reckons ya right, rabbit stew, me favourite. 'Tas bin a while since I've 'ad one of ya Aunt Clara's famous rabbit stews. When do ya two go back to the States?" "Three weeks,"

said Maddy. "I wish we could stay longer." "I 'spect ya missin' ya folks though?" "Of course Tom, but the time here has gone so quickly and it will be at least another year before we come back." "Aah a year ain't nothin'; you'll be back 'ere afore ya know it. Anyhow's, I 'spect ya mum an' dad are really missin' ya both." "Yes they are," said Maddy, "we phone them every three days but we couldn't speak to mum last time we phoned." "Why wos that?" "Dad said something about mum working extra shifts at the hospital, something to do with an outbreak of a flu bug or something like that." "Oh that sounds a bit serious, hope ya mum is gonna be ok. 'Tis a good thing that ya mum 'as fairy magic protectin' 'er." "Are we protected by fairy magic Tom?" enquired Maddy. "Oh for sure, since the day ya were born." "Lunch is ready," called Clara.

As usual, Jamie was the first to sit at the table. "Smells wonderful," said Tom. The twins watched as Tom cleared his plate, mopping up the last remnants of the stew with a thick slice of Clara's homemade bread. "Would you like some more Tom?" asked Clara. "No thank ye Clara, I'm full ta burstin'." The twins chuckled. "That wos a fine meal Clara, fit for a king! I couldn' eat another morsel" "Oh that's a shame," said Clara, "I've made rhubarb crumble with custard for afters." "Rhubarb crumble ya say? Me favourite, p'raps I could manage just a small bit?" "I thought you might," laughed Clara.

She waited until everyone had finished before ordering them into the other room, so that she could clear up. Tom didn't need asking twice. He was too full to do anything, other than sit down in a comfortable chair. Jamie and Maddy could talk of nothing but the forthcoming visit. Tom did his best to look interested, but with a full belly, it was as much as he could do to stay awake. Maddy signalled to Jamie that Tom had actually dozed off, placing her finger to her lips. She then pointed to the door, beckoning to Jamie that they should leave Tom in peace. Quietly, they made their way back to the kitchen and Aunt Clara. They explained that Tom had fallen asleep. "He works very hard on his farm," said Clara. "I don't suppose for one minute he gets many home cooked meals, it's good that he can relax. There's no need to wake him because he's coming with us when we leave. He's going to walk with us to the woods." "Is he coming to the village with us?" asked Jamie. "No my dear, he hasn't been invited and our little friends can be a bit funny about things like that. Anyway, Tom will want to be getting home to his pigs."

The afternoon seemed, to the twins, to drag by. Jamie kept looking at his watch, informing his sister every fifteen minutes or so, what the time was and that it would be hours before their visit. Maddy suggested doing some magic to pass away the hours before tea, knowing that once it was finished, they would be heading for the fairy village. Strangely enough, the time did indeed seem to pass more quickly whilst practicing their new found skills. In fact, it seemed that, in no time at all, Aunt Clara was calling them in for tea. "Go and give Tom a call." "Is he still asleep?" asked a rather surprised Maddy. "He is indeed," replied Clara. "Tom, Tom wake up," whispered Maddy, not wishing to startle him. "Oh dear," said Tom as he mustered from his slumber, "I musta dozed off for a minute there." Maddy informed him that he had actually been asleep all the afternoon. Tom looked a trifle embarrassed. "Tha's not like me," he said. "Aunt Clara told us to let you sleep, you must have been tired. Anyway, tea is ready."

Entering the kitchen, Tom apologised to Clara. "Nonsense Tom, there's no need to apologise. I often feel the need for a nap in the afternoon; I suppose it comes with age." As usual, the table was laid with an abundance of food. "Help yourselves," said Clara, "oh and I've made an extra batch of cakes Tom, I thought you might like to take them home with you." Tom couldn't answer because his mouth was full. Swallowing quickly, he thanked Clara. "What time do ya wanna be goin'?" asked Tom. "About seven if that's alright, I don't want us being late and it's very nice of you to escort us Tom." "'Tis the least I kin do after the wunderful day I've 'ad. 'Tis much appreciated, it's made a luvly change to sit an' eat a fine meal in the comp'nee of good friens." "We've all enjoyed today Tom," said Clara. "We should do it more often." "Tha'll be great, I'd very much like tha'," said Tom. "Then that's settled, from now on Tom, every week you must come over for dinner, shall we say Sunday?" "Aye … tha'll be great," stuttered Tom." Yes, the twins were right. Tom and Clara definitely had a soft spot for one another. "My goodness," said Clara, "just look at the time! We must think about clearing up, we need to leave in about half an hour. We certainly don't want to be late now, do we?" "I'll help," said Maddy as she began to clear away the dirty dishes from the table. "'Ow's 'bout young Jamie an' me wipin' up for ya Clara?" "Well that's very kind of you Tom, but you're a guest." "Guest? Be blowed! 'Tis the least I can do, now pass me them dryin' cloths." Within no time the kitchen was spotless, just the way Clara liked it. "Don't forget your cakes Tom; I've put them in a tin for you." "Thank ye kindly Clara, I'll sees ya git the tin back." "There's no hurry." Clara told the twins to fetch a jacket each, Jamie arguing that the weather didn't warrant it. "I agree," said Aunt Clara, "but it might be chilly when we return, best be on the safe side." Maddy agreed. "We had best be making tracks," said Tom, "'tis almost seven."

CHAPTER ELEVEN

The Fairy Village

Reaching the spot in the woods where they were to meet Wickit, Clara told everyone to be on their guard. "For what?" asked Jamie. "Anything out of the ordinary." "Such as?" "Spies watching us." "Spies!" stuttered Maddy. "Oh yeah, these 'ere woods are full of spies."

said Tom, "Nasty little things, I've seen 'em scurryin' 'bout in the undergrowth. Nearly shot one once, thought 'twas a rabbit." "What was it?" enquired Jamie. "Don't rightly know, thinks it was a troll or goblin, ugly lookin' thing, that's for sure." "Thank you for waiting with us Tom," said Clara. "These woods can be a bit spooky at night. I'm sure Wickit will be along any minute, it's not like him to be late." Suddenly something caught the corner of Tom's eye. "I do believe our little friend 'as arrived," he said. The twins looked around to try and see the tiny fairy. "We can't see him," said Maddy. "Come on Wickit, we know you're there," said Clara. At that moment, a bright light shone out from nowhere and hovered just above Clara. It was like a tiny orb. "Hello there Wickit, we were wondering where you had got to." Wickit told Clara that he had actually arrived before them to make sure it was safe. A flash of light and there before them stood Wickit. "It's nice to see you Tom." "Ya too," replied Tom, "but now you're 'ere I s'pose I best be gittin' off 'ome. Give me regards to King Peteron an' 'is family." "Will do Tom."

They waited until Tom was out of sight then Wickit suggested that they should also make haste. Clara agreed. Wickit told the trio to stand close together, and then he circled above them three times sprinkling tiny particles of fairy dust from his wings down upon them. The twins just stood there, having no idea what would happen next. They watched in amazement as the forest seemed to light up and there, before them, was a beautiful glowing archway. Mesmerized, they stood silently as they could see the fairy village through the arch. Wickit appeared in front of them. "Follow me."

Clara and the twins followed Wickit through the arch, and then something very strange seemed to happen. Once inside the fairy village, Wickit didn't appear to be so small; in fact nothing did. Maddy couldn't help but wonder whether they had shrunk, or whether Wickit had got bigger. Judging by the baffled look on Jamie's face, he was having the very same thought! The village was a hive of activity; everybody seemed to be doing something. Directly in front of them was what appeared to be a school, with the tiny fairy children sitting, crossed legged, on the ground, being taught by a very beautiful fairy girl. Jamie couldn't take his eyes off her. Maddy, however, was far more interested in the archery lesson which was going on at the far end of the village. Young fairies, both male and female, were being taught archery skills and from what Maddy had observed, they were very accurate and fast. She witnessed at least four bull's eyes.

The twins were so engrossed watching, that neither one noticed the arrival of King Peteron and his family. Clara nudged Jamie, who in turn nudged Maddy. As the King introduced himself to the twins, Maddy thought what a kind face he had, but his huge eyes were hiding a deep sadness behind them. She remembered what Aunt Clara had told her about the death of his beloved Queen. As the King's children introduced themselves, Maddy found herself feeling very comfortable with them. She especially liked Prince Iandrew; he had a certain calmness about him, but with the look of a warrior, bold and handsome. No doubt he would one day make a fine King.

After the introductions King Peteron told Clara that Nanamic wished to see her. He told Wickit to give the twins a guided tour of the village, so that everyone could meet them. The King looked a bit agitated when the Princess Melissa asked if she could accompany the twins. Reluctantly he agreed and Wickit looked pleased.

CHAPTER TWELVE

Nanamic the Wise

"I'm going to have to keep my eye on those two," said Peteron, referring to Wickit and Melissa. "Oh I'm sure there's no harm in their friendship," said Clara, "they're young that's all." "If only my instincts told me that Clara, I would not worry so much. I myself would welcome Wickit as a suitor for Melissa's hand. I am extremely fond of him. I already think of him as my son, but I know their union could never be, the council of elders would never allow it. Sadly, Wickit is not of royal blood and I have no wish to see Melissa carrying the burden of a broken heart, as I have done all these years." Clara gently patted Peteron's shoulder. "Is there no way the council will allow it?"she asked. "There is only one way. That is for Wickit to forfeit his own life for Melissa. Knowing that he would, as I do, is simply not enough. Alas, if it did ever come to pass, Wickit would probably die. It is not something we can arrange, it would be purely down to chance."

"There you are, I was beginning to think you had forgotten me." Clara looked up. "Nanamic, my dear friend! How are you?" "I am well Clara and yourself?"

"I too am well thank you Nanamic, apart from my aching bones. Unfortunately, it's simply something us more mature humans have to endure." The friends laughed. King Peteron asked Nanamic if he could be excused as there was much he needed to do. "Of course," said Nanamic, "Clara and I have a lot to catch up on." "I will see you before you leave Clara," said Peteron. "Shall we go inside Clara; I've made us some of your tea." "That would be lovely. I've brought you a small gift Nanamic." Feeling inside her jacket, "Ah there it is," said Clara. She passed Nanamic a jar of fresh honey. The old fairy clapped her hands together with excitement. "How kind of you Clara, it's my favourite thing." "I know, that's why I bring you some every time I come."

"How is Tom? Are his pigs doing alright?" "That's a strange thing to ask," said Clara. "Yes, Tom and his pigs are doing just fine." "Oh that's good." "Is everything alright Nanamic? Tom tells me that he's been seeing and hearing strange things in the woods at night." "I've no doubt he has." "What's going on?" asked Clara. "Truth is Clara, we're not absolutely sure, but we fear it may be Stigamites. The noises and lights that Tom has been hearing and seeing are our scouts. Fortunately, we had not seen or heard anything until yesterday." "Why did you think anything was wrong, and what happened yesterday?" "Our elders and I had sensed an evil presence for several days, so we consulted our Oracle. It confirmed our fears, so we have all had to be extra vigilant." "What are Stigamites?" "They are pure evil, demonic creatures." "What, like Bawllows?" "Far worse my dear, Bawllows are far less of a worry than Stigamites." "Are they like them though?" "To tell you the truth Clara, we don't actually know. We know that Bawllows are fairies gone bad, but we really don't know about Stigamites. They seem to have some similarities to Bawllows, but nobody really knows. The most likely explanation is that they come from demons of the underworld, who cannot live in the normal world; they have to live deep down in the ground."

"So why are they here?" "We believe that because their masters cannot walk on this green earth, they send Stigamites to wreak havoc upon it, to try and find a way for them to come among us and live in the light, as we do. Stories from our past tell of fairies being taken by them never to be seen again. Our worst fear is that they will try and take our Oracle." "Why would they want your Oracle?" "Because it holds great power and if that power were to fall into the wrong hands, the consequences would be devastating. The world as we know it would be gone forever. A terrible darkness would befall the land and most living things would die, so you can see why we are so concerned." But what happened yesterday Nanamic?" "Mina, the elf queen, requested a meeting with me." "But I thought that fairies and elves didn't get along?" "We don't, but where serious issues are concerned, we tend to bury our differences and believe me Clara, Stigamites are a very serious issue. They pose the same threat to all woodland dwellers; fairies, pixies, elves, goblins and trolls alike, even Bawllows fear them. So you see my dear Clara, we must, under these circumstances, work together." "What! Even creatures like Bawllows!" "Unfortunately even Bawllows, although we would hope it will never come to that, but with an enemy so terrible, it pays to have as many allies as you can."

"I remember Dragonscott from when I was a child." "Sadly my dear Clara, so do we all, especially the King. His life changed for ever that terrible day and I know that he would love to kill Dragonscott for what he did, but now is not the time. There are more important things to deal with, although do not, for one minute, think that there could ever be an alliance between us, it's just that Dragonscott and his followers pose no threat to us while Stigamites are here. He fears them the same as us and any information he can give us regarding them would be welcomed." "So tell me what Mina said." "She told me that two nights ago, a Stigamite tried to take an elf child." "Why?" "We don't really know, maybe for food." "Nanamic! You cannot be serious, they wouldn't really eat a child," said Clara, "that's so terrible." "Indeed it's a terrible thought, but nevertheless, we believe it may have been the reason, so you see Clara, why we fear them so. The elf child in question is now desperately ill with a fever, due to the Stigamites bite. They carry a lethal poison. I gave Mina a potion to give to the child; hopefully it was not administered too late. Which brings me to give you this." Nanamic handed Clara a small bag; inside were two tiny bottles full of liquid. Nanamic instructed Clara to give the bottles to Tom. Clara asked what they were for. Nanamic explained that Tom should sprinkle a few drops into his pigs' food and that would protect them from the Stigamites' bite, should they attack his farm. "Oh my goodness!" gasped Clara, "Will they attack humans?" "Not normally, but we don't want to take any chances now do we?" smiled Nanamic. "It's highly unlikely that humans will ever see a Stigamite, they only move about at night. However, the council and I feel that people such as yourself and Tom could be slightly at risk because of your connection to us. That is why I am giving you these things. I've put some other useful things in the bag for you Clara."

Placing her hand back inside the bag, Clara pulled out four tiny charms in the shape of a star, each secured on a silver chain. "Those are for the twins, yourself and Tom, one each." "What are they for?" asked Clara. "They will give you some protection should you run into any of our horrid little friends; there's also a small amulet in the bag, secure it to your front door. That should help to ward off any unwelcome guests and last, but by no means least, the envelope inside the bag contains some healing powders which you may find will come in useful within the farming community." "How so? asked Clara. "Well, if any animal should receive a bite from a Stigamite, they would be unlikely to recover from it and alas, your human medicine would be of little use. We all know that the villagers call upon you Clara, in such times, so we thought it best to prepare you." "Why would a Stigamite attack livestock? Surely they pose no threat?" "You are quite right my dear, but they do feed off them, blood suckers no less and once their teeth pierce the skin, the poison is released." "How do I use the powder?" "Simply add a tiny pinch to some water and mix into a paste, and then pack the puncture holes with it. With luck and fairy magic you will save a life.

Now let's talk about nicer things. I understand the twins are doing excellently with their new found gifts. No doubt, in time, they will be an asset to us fairy folk. Wickit tells me that they are quick learners." "Indeed they are Nanamic. Jamie is so eager to learn, especially magic. Maddy seems to be more like Sally, very much the sceptic at first, but definitely more than a match for that brother of hers. It's been wonderful having them both here, but the time seems to be flying by. I'll miss them when they have to go back." "Perhaps they won't be returning to America as soon as you think Clara." "Unfortunately Nanamic, their flights are already booked and I dare say John and Sally are dead keen for them to return." "I agree with you Clara, but sometimes things are taken out of our hands and plans have to be changed." "Are you trying to tell me something Nanamic, nothing bad is going to happen is it?" "Good heavens no Clara, but we understand that there is a terrible virus in America at present, a type of flu I believe." "Yes, Sally did mention something about a flu type bug when we spoke to her last and it is claiming many lives. At present there is no cure, so you see America is not a safe place." "But surely the twins would be fine; they seem to have a natural immunity to illness like Sally and I." "Yes I know, but my senses tell me that America is taking it all very seriously and I believe that if it is not contained soon, they will close the airports and docks. Nobody will be able to get in or out." "Oh that's terrible," stated Clara, "the twins will be upset, and although I must admit it would be nice if they could stay longer, I just wish it was under happier circumstances." "As do we all. However, in the meantime Clara, best not to mention it to anyone, it's not yet official." "Nanamic," smiled Clara, "I have known you far too long, that if it wasn't going to happen you would not have told me, but I will keep it to myself."

The twins were having a whale of a time. One of the archers asked Jamie if he would like to have a go with a bow. As ever, Jamie was only too keen to accept the offer. Artex the archer first showed Jamie how to hold and position the bow, then placing an arrow, explained that to improve his aim, Jamie should gently touch his chin with the arrow shaft, at the same time keeping a firm grip between his two fingers at the tail end. When Artex was satisfied with Jamie's position, he instructed him to draw back as much as he could on the bow string and when he felt ready, to release the arrow. Jamie followed the instructions, then without the slightest hesitation, released the arrow. "Well done!" exclaimed a rather surprised Artex, as he looked at the target. Jamie had hit the ring just outside the bull's eye. Maddy and the others began to clap. "He's a natural!" yelled Wickit. The other fairies, who had been watching, nodded their heads in agreement. "Wanna try again?" asked Artex. "You bet!" replied Jamie. This time, Jamie needed no instruction. Within seconds he was ready to fire. He noticed that the other archers who had been practising on other targets had stopped to watch him. He felt a little nervous at this, but told himself that he could do as well as before, if not better. Taking a deep breath, he pulled back hard on the bow and released the arrow. "Bulls eye!" cheered Artex. Jamie blushed, although inside he felt an overwhelming sense of satisfaction.

As Maddy watched her brother, Melissa told her that female fairies also learn self defence. In fact her sister, Princess Bellaruth was as good as many of the men when it came to it, especially when it came to swordsmanship. Undoubtedly she could hold her own against most warriors, even Prince Iandrew. "Really?" said Maddy, as she smiled over at the prince. "Actually, I only let her think she has beaten me," he said. "You know how girls get when they lose; it's just easier to let them think they've won." "Oh really," quipped Bellaruth. "I think not dear brother; you just won't admit that I'm as good as you." "Now now children," said Princess Michelalena sarcastically. Maddy and Melissa laughed. "Would you like to see some of our animals," said Wickit, trying desperately to change the subject before a full scale argument erupted between Iandrew and Bellaruth. "Oh yes please, I love animals," said Maddy. "I'm hoping to be a vet one day." "I'm sure you'll make a very good vet," said Michelalena. "You have a kind heart, which I feel, sadly, is something that not all humans possess." Maddy thanked Michelalena for the compliment and at that very moment, she knew why Aunt Clara held the princess in such high esteem. There was a wonderful kindness about Michelalena, the way she spoke in a soft voice and indeed as Clara had said, she was a real beauty. Maddy could sense that she held all living things as precious. Clara was right; there was not a mean bone in Michelalena's body. Maddy also noticed that her sisters were far more outspoken and far more at ease with her and Jamie, but something inside told Maddy that, given the time to get to know Michelalena, their friendship would last a lifetime. Yes, Maddy had made up her mind that Michelalena was indeed everything Aunt Clara had said, a truly kind and wonderful fairy.

Wickit called to Jamie to ask if he wanted to go with them to see the animals. "No thanks," called Jamie, "I'll stay with Artex if that's ok?" "I'll take good care of him," called Artex. As the party set off to see the animals, Maddy noticed that Wickit never left Melissa's side; they laughed and joked with each other. By contrast, Bellaruth and Iandrew were still squabbling over who was the best swordsman. Michelalena talked to Maddy about the animals, telling her of the baby fawn that had been born just two weeks ago. "I've nicknamed him Wobbler." "Why? asked Maddy. "Simply because when I first saw him, he could barely stand and he kept falling over." "Oh dear," said Maddy, "is he ok now?" "Absolutely!" said Michelalena. "He's running about like a hare." They both chuckled.

They approached the part of the village where the animals were kept, to be greeted by an older male fairy. He had a round, plump, happy face; his hair was pure white. Maddy liked him instantly. Wickit introduced him as Link, explaining that Link had a very important job tending to all the animals and that no-one in the village knew as much about animals as he did. Wickit told Link that Maddy was Clara's niece. "I heard they were going to visit, how is Clara?" he asked, looking at Maddy. "She's well, thank you." "I'm pleased to hear that, she's a good sort is Clara. Isn't there supposed to be another one, a boy?" asked Link. "You mean young Jamie. Well, he's busy taking archery lessons with Artex, but I'm sure he'll be along later."

Link looked at Michelalena, "I expect you've come to see how that young fawn is doing?" "We have," said the princess, "if it's possible." "Oh I'm sure he'll be only too pleased to see you, let me call him." Link put his thumb and finger into his mouth and blew out a high pitched whistle. Everyone waited silently. Moments later, they heard a rustling sound coming from the woods. A large stag appeared, cautiously and slowly making its way towards them. Link called to it not to be afraid, that Maddy meant him no harm. As the stag came closer, Maddy held out her hand and in a gentle voice, beckoned the beast to her. She gently reached over and stroked his head. "Oh you're so beautiful!" she whispered. The stag raised his head then banged his hoof three times on the ground. Within seconds another deer appeared, a female and next to her stood a tiny fawn. "Come on," said Michelalena, "don't be shy; no one is going to hurt you." The tiny fawn made his way over to Michelalena under the watchful eyes of his parents. Michelalena threw her arms around his neck. "My, you have grown since I last saw you and you're very handsome." The fawn nuzzled his head on the princess's shoulder. Maddy noticed that other animals had come out of the forest; there were rabbits and squirrels, mice, even a fox and her cubs, which made no attempt to chase the rabbits.

"If you sit down on the ground, they'll come over to you," said Link. He was right, no sooner had Maddy sat down when a young squirrel ran up her arm. They stayed with Link and the animals for a long time, and then Prince Iandrew suggested that they should be getting back. They each thanked Link for letting them stay. He seemed to Maddy to be a trifle embarrassed, especially when Michelalena kissed him on the cheek. "Look after Wobbler," she said, as they made their way back to the others.

Maddy couldn't wait to tell Aunt Clara and Jamie about her wonderful time with the animals. Jamie had his own story to tell about how he had learnt to use a sword and a catapult and that Artex thought that one day, Jamie would become a great warrior, such as himself. "Are you two nearly ready to go?" They hadn't noticed Aunt Clara. She was standing with King Peteron and Nanamic. "Oh, can't we stay a bit longer?" pleaded Jamie. "I think we've been here long enough," said Clara, "and we don't want to outstay our welcome, do we?" King Peteron told the twins that they could return to the village before they went home, adding that perhaps next time, he and Nanamic could spend some time with them. Then he instructed Wickit to see them safely home.

It was the same routine as earlier. Wickit flew above them sprinkling fairy dust on them and just as before, the forest appeared to open. As they made their way to the arch, they waved and called goodbye to their new found friends. Once back in the forest, the arch simply vanished. Wickit went ahead to ensure that the way was safe. Before they knew it, they were back at Clara's cottage. They thanked Wickit for seeing them safely home and for giving them such a wonderful time. "You're most welcome," he called as he flew up into the evening sky. "I'll see you all soon, goodbye." "Take care Wickit," called Clara. "I think I'll put the kettle on and make us some supper, and then you two can tell me all about your day." "Supper?" said Jamie. "We had supper before we left, it must be nearly time for breakfast." Aunt Clara laughed. "Oh my dear Jamie, I completely forgot to tell you. Time is different inside the fairy village. We've barely been gone an hour in human time. Look at the clock; it's only just past eight o'clock." "No way," said Jamie, "we've been gone hours." "It seems that way, but as I said, time there is different. It took your mother and me many years to get used to it."

Clara told Maddy to make the tea while she sorted out something for supper. Jamie's job was to lay the table. In no time at all, the three of them were sitting down eating and telling Aunt Clara about the fantastic time they had at the fairy village. In fact, they didn't stop talking until it was time for bed. Clara had given them the star charms that Nanamic had given to her. She told the twins to wear them at all times and that they would be taking Tom's one to him in the morning. She explained about the Stigamites, but insisted that they shouldn't worry as they had fairy protection. Maddy told Clara that she had made something for the little piglet, Apple, which she would take to Tom's in the morning if Clara thought he wouldn't mind. Clara assured her that Tom wouldn't mind, in fact quite the opposite, he would probably find it quite flattering, especially as he was keeping the piglet as a pet.

CHAPTER THIRTEEN

Stigamites at Tom's Farm

Walking to Tom's farm, the twins were still telling each other about their time spent at the fairy village. Neither of them could wait to tell Tom. As they went through his gate, they all noticed how quiet the farm seemed. Clara called out to Tom but there was no reply. She called again, this time Tom called back. "I'm in the barn, cum quick!"

His voice sounded panic stricken. Hurriedly, they made their way to the barn. "What's wrong Tom?" asked Clara as she spotted him crouching down in the straw amongst his pigs."Sumthin' is up wi' me animals Clara, 'smorning I foun' three o' me chickins dead an' me poor old sow 'ere ain't doin' much betta." "Isn't that Apple's mother," said Maddy, referring to the sow that Tom was tending. "Ah 'tis," replied Tom, with a sad look on his face. "What's wrong with her?" asked Jamie. "Don't rightly know, I've not come across anythin' like it," replied Tom. "One things fa sure, if I don't soon find out, she's gonna end up like me chickins!" "Has she got any marks on her? asked Clara. "Funny you should ask me that," said Tom, "I did notice a couple a tiny marks, thought p'raps the other pigs may 'ave had a go at 'er." "Let me see," said Clara. Carefully, she checked the sow and sure enough, there were tiny puncture marks. "Quick Maddy, pass me that envelope out of my bag, the one that Nanamic gave me."

Carefully, Maddy passed Clara the envelope. "Tom, you get me some water and something small that I can mix up a paste in." "What is it?" he asked. "I think it might be Stigamites," replied Clara. "What on earth are

Stigamites?" said Tom. "I'll tell you later, but first, we must try and save this sow, so hurry up and fetch me the water." Moments later Tom handed Clara a bucket of water and an old tin mug for mixing. He watched as Clara took a small pinch of powder from the envelope and carefully mixed it in the mug with a little water. It sizzled like fizzy lemonade, and then Clara gently pressed tiny amounts of the paste into the puncture wounds on the sow's side. "Now we wait, I just hope we're in time," she said. Tom looked puzzled.

Clara told him to go to the house and make them all a cup of tea. She would stay and watch over the sow. Shortly, Tom returned with a tray of tea. As they drank, Clara told him all about the Stigamites and the danger they posed to livestock; in fact the reason for them being there that very morning was to give Tom the things that Nanamic had sent. "Looks like ya got 'ere in the nick o' time," he said. "P'raps I best be puttin' some of them drops inta me animal feed, don't want any others endin' up like 'er," he said, pointing to the sow. "Good idea Tom and put your charm on as well." "I will," replied Tom. They all stayed in the barn watching for any sign of improvement in the sow.

While they waited, the twins told Tom all about their time in the fairy village. Maddy told Tom that she had made something for Apple. She passed Tom a small bag. "Now wot might tha' be?" he said. Tom pulled out a tiny silver ball, a piece of leather strapping pulled through it. "It's a necklace," said Maddy. "Will he be allowed to wear it?" "I don' see why not, if the leather fits round 'is neck." Maddy told Tom that she used to have two of the little silver balls, until one broke off and was lost. They were from a necklace she used to wear. She swapped the chain for the leather strapping, so that the little piglet could have it. Also the ball could be opened, so she had written Apple's name and the address of the farm on a piece of paper and placed it inside. That way, if he ever got lost someone could bring him home. Tom went into the pen where the little piglet was and tied the leather strap around his neck. "My, don't 'e look grand," said Tom. He opened the pen so that Apple could go over to Maddy, which he did without hesitation. "There'll be no stoppin' 'im now," laughed Tom.

Several hours passed then Clara noticed that the sow started to move, slowly at first as if she were waking from a deep sleep, then suddenly, without warning, the sow scrambled to her feet and hurried towards the pen where her piglets were. "Well I'll be blessed," said Tom, as he opened the pen allowing her to enter. "'Tis a miracle Clara, I thought fa sure she was gonna die." He told Maddy to put Apple back in with the sow. "Tha' fairy medicine sure is powerful stuff!" "It certainly is," replied Clara with a chuckle.

Clara invited Tom back to the cottage for lunch. He declined, stating that it was probably best if he stayed with the pigs, just to be on the safe side. Clara told Tom that they would return the next day to check on him and to find out how the sow was doing. As the twins and Aunt Clara made their way back to the cottage, Jamie asked Clara if she thought Tom's animals would be okay now. She could see no reason why they shouldn't be, after all, the medicine seemed to work on the sow and the drops Nanamic had given Tom to put on their food should stop any further deaths from Stigamite bites. "I wonder why they attacked Tom's farm," said Maddy. "Perhaps Nanamic was right about us being more at risk because of our connections with the fairy folk," replied Clara. "Let's just hope we ourselves don't have any trouble with them."

As they made their way back through the woods, Maddy noticed that Aunt Clara seemed to be slightly on edge and asked what was wrong. "Oh it's probably nothing," reassured Clara. "I think that what happened at Tom's today has unsettled me a bit that's all." "What was that?" said Jamie. "I didn't hear anything," said Maddy. "Well I did! There it goes again!" snapped Jamie. The three of them stood quietly, the sun was filtering through the trees. There was little or no breeze, in fact the woods were much quieter than normal. As they stood there listening for what Jamie had heard, a strange eeriness seemed to surround them and a cold chill ran down Clara's spine. Just as Clara was about to tell the twins to continue on their journey, a strange sound distracted her. It was not a sound that was familiar to her, a sort of low pitched growl coming from down in the undergrowth. The twins could also hear it. "What's that?" asked Jamie in a quiet voice. Clara replied that she had not heard it before, but her instincts were telling her that something was most definitely wrong. "I feel like something is watching us," said a rather frightened Maddy. Clara too, felt that there were many eyes watching them from the undergrowth. She ordered that the twins pull their necklace charms to the outside of their clothes, so that they could be seen. "Do you think it's Stigamites?" gasped Maddy. Clara did not answer her; instead she signalled to her to be quiet. The twins stood silently as Clara chanted a fairy spell,

FAIRY GOODNESS, FAIRY TRUE, TO LIGHT OUR WAY WE CALL ON YOU, MAY EVIL FLEE AND LET US PASS, FOR YOUR PROTECTION WE NOW ASK.

Suddenly, the woods seemed to light up, tiny voices seemed to echo from all around. Without warning, the undergrowth seemed to come alive as though it had hundreds of tiny creatures moving within it. Strange noises, like screams and grunts could be heard, but the twins and Clara could see nothing and as quickly as it began, it ended. "What the hell was that?" exclaimed Jamie. A familiar voice answered him. It was Prince Iandrew. Within a second, he was hovering above them, quickly followed by Wickit, Artex and many of the fairy warriors. "Thank goodness," sighed Clara, "for a moment there, I thought we were done for." "My father sent us." said the Prince. "He heard your chant Clara. We have been watching the woods very closely for several days now. It's not very safe for you and the children to be wandering about out here now. Nanamic thinks you would be safer if you took the long route to Tom's and avoided the woods." Clara agreed that, in future, they would drive to Tom's farm. Wickit told them that he and Artex would see them safely back. Clara told them about the attack on Tom's farm and that the potions which Nanamic had given to her had indeed saved the sow's life. Prince Iandrew told them that he must return to the village to report this news. "Take care, be alert!" he called, as he disappeared into the trees.

As they reached Clara's cottage, Wickit and Artex told Clara and the twins to wait outside while they checked inside to ensure that it was safe to enter. Minutes later they gave the all clear. Still slightly shaken, Clara thought that a nice cup of tea was in order. "Good idea," said Wickit, "allow me!" Within a flash, there was the tea tray on the table in front of Clara and the twins, a pot of fresh, piping hot tea just waiting to be poured. "Thank you Wickit," said Clara. "I'm sure we'll all feel better once we've had a nice cuppa." The two tiny fairies stood on the table. Maddy asked them if the horrible things in the woods were Stigamites. "Seems likely," replied Wickit. Would they have hurt us?" asked Maddy. "Hard to say, they have never been known to attack humans directly, but as Nanamic has been saying, these Stigamites don't appear to behave according to type." "How so?" enquired Clara. "Well, take your little run in with them today, very unusual, what with it being broad daylight and all. They have never been known to move about in the daylight hours, they've always attacked at night." "Do you think the children are safe here?" asked a rather worried looking

91

Clara. "Oh for sure," said Artex. "The charms Nanamic gave you should keep them away and your cottage is protected by fairy magic as you know Clara, but, as always in these situations, you should be extra vigilant, keep all your doors and windows locked at night and you can always call upon us." "That's very reassuring," said Clara. "Be sure to thank Prince Iandrew and the others for us, we were very grateful for your help." "No need for thanks," said Wickit. "As always Clara, it's a pleasure to help you, but now we really must return to our village, or Melissa will be sending out a search party to find us," chuckled Wickit. "I'm sure she will," said Clara, "she's very fond of you, as are we all." The tiny fairy blushed. "We will keep an eye on you," said Artex but now, we really must bid you all farewell." The tiny men flew up towards the ceiling and then in a flash of light, they both disappeared. "Goodbye," called Clara and the twins.

"Well I suppose I should be getting us some lunch," said Clara. "Perhaps we'll just make do with some sandwiches and cakes. I'll cook something proper this evening." Fifteen minutes later the three of them were tucking into cheese sandwiches, followed by a large slab of Victoria sponge. "I see our encounter with Stigamites hasn't spoilt your appetite Jamie!" laughed Clara, as her young nephew helped himself to another slice of cake. "What are we doing this afternoon?" asked Maddy. "Well," said Clara "I think it would be a good idea if we brushed up on the magic and potions that you two have been learning and perhaps now would be a good time for the pair of you to learn some fairy chants. Can you remember the one I used today?" Clara was impressed to hear that they could both remember what she had chanted. She was even more impressed when they both repeated the chant word perfect.

CHAPTER FOURTEEN
The Telegram

The following week seemed to pass without any problems. Aunt Clara taught the twins how to chant magic spells and, as usual, they picked everything up with no trouble. Wickit was a regular visitor to the cottage. King Peteron insisted that he keep an eye on them. The Stigamites appeared to be lying low; there had been no other reported attacks. Indeed, life in the English countryside seemed to be as uneventful as ever. That was until the postman arrived with a telegram from America. It read, 'children cannot return. No flights. Must stay in England. Please phone. Sally. "Oh dear," said Aunt Clara, "it would appear that something is wrong and that you two will be staying here a while longer." "Are mum and dad okay?" asked a rather worried looking Maddy? "Yes my dear," replied Clara, "they're fine, it's the airports. It would appear that there are no flights into America." "What on earth could have happened?" asked Jamie, his voice quite panic stricken. Clara decided to tell them what Nanamic had told her, she could see no point in them worrying any longer. "Do you think that's what it is Aunt Clara?"asked

Maddy. "I would imagine so," said Clara, "but there's only one way to find out for sure and that's to phone Sally today. We'll drive into the village this afternoon and call her; perhaps we can make it a round trip and pop in to see Tom. I'll take him some jam and you two can take those stale leftover cakes for his pigs. I'm sure Apple and his family would like them."

The lady in the post office asked Clara if everything was alright. She had taken the earlier telegram. Clara explained that they were going to phone America now and that was their reason for being there. Connecting to the States always seemed to take ages, today being no exception. "Hello Sally, is that you? We received your telegram this morning." Sally explained everything; it was just as Nanamic had said. The virus had claimed many lives so the American government had declared a state of quarantine. Nobody was allowed in or out of America. They had their top scientist working round the clock to find an antidote. Sally felt confident that it would only be a short time before everything would be back to normal and the twins could return home. Clara told Sally that it would be wonderful for the twins to stay with her for a bit longer. She would try to register them in the local school, as it would probably be several weeks before they could return home. Sally agreed that it was a good idea. When Clara and Sally had sorted everything out, Jamie and Maddy spoke to their mum on the phone. Jamie's first thought was to protest about having to go to school; why couldn't they just stay with Aunt Clara as before? Sally explained that Clara could get into trouble if they didn't go to school. Sally told the twins that she would write them a long letter. She had no concerns about leaving them to stay longer with Clara. She knew how well looked after they were and despite having to go to school, she knew that, deep down, they were both having a wonderful time. They all said their goodbyes, and then Clara hung up the phone. She asked the post mistress how much she owed for the call, then proceeded to tell her about the terrible virus in America. As they left the post office the lady handed the twins an ice lolly each, checking first with Clara that they were allowed to have them. Clara told her that she was very kind and that she was sure the twins would welcome such a treat on such a hot day.

In the car on the way to Tom's, all Jamie did was moan about having to go to school. "We're supposed to be on vacation," he mumbled. Clara explained that they would not be going to school for at least another two weeks, because the schools in England had a different holiday system to America and that the school term would not begin until then at least .Who knows, by then, everything in America might be back to normal and they could return home. Hearing this Jamie's spirits were slightly lifted.

As they pulled into Tom's farm, Clara honked the horn. Tom appeared within seconds. "Hello," called Clara. Tom walked over to where Clara had parked and being a gentleman, he opened the car door for her. "'Tis a nice surprise," said Tom, "funny thing is Clara, I were just thinkin' about yer." "Were you now?" replied Clara, with a slightly flushed look on her face. "Why would you be thinking of me?" "Tell yer the truth Clara, I were thinkin' 'ow nice 'tis been these past weeks, what with you an' the twins poppin' over and me comin' round for Sundee lunch. I've never really been much of a one for comp'nee, I s'pose it's me old age creepin' up on me. One thing's fa sure, I like it and I'll miss the twins when they go 'ome." "Well actually Tom, they're not going home for probably a few more weeks," said Clara. "How so?" asked Tom. Clara explained about the terrible virus that was spreading through America. Seeing that the twins were looking a bit disappointed, Tom tried to lift their spirits by telling them that at least they could see Apple grow bigger and that maybe Maddy could teach him some simple tricks. The thought of this seemed to please the twins. "Do you really think he could learn tricks?" asked Maddy. "I don' see why not," said Tom, "arter all, 'e's a smart little fella."

Clara and Tom went into the farmhouse, the twins headed for the barn. Time always seemed to fly by when they were at the farm. In fact it seemed to the twins that no time at all had passed, when Clara was calling to them to say cheerio to Apple, as it was time to leave. As usual, Aunt Clara asked Tom if he would like to join them for supper. Normally he would decline the offer, except on Sundays, but on this occasion, he readily accepted. Tom told Clara that he would follow her in his truck, that way Clara would not have the inconvenience of having to drive him home later. Clara would never agree to Tom walking home through the woods. Jamie asked if he could ride in the truck with Tom. "Course ya can," said Tom, "I'd be glad of ya comp'nee." "Shall we go then?" said Clara. "Maddy and I will get supper started so don't be too long you two. "We'll be right be'ind ya," said Tom. "I'll just check me pigs afore we leave, young Jamie 'ere can give me an 'and."

As Clara and Maddy pulled out of the yard, Tom and Jamie headed off towards the barn. "See you both in a while," called Clara, as she drove out of sight. Back in the barn, Jamie helped Tom check that the pigs had enough water and food for the afternoon. Jamie noticed that Tom kept talking about Clara, telling him what a grand lady she is and that he had no doubt that she was the best cook in the village. Even on the drive back to Clara's, Tom talked of nothing else.

"Somethin' smells good," said Tom, as they walked through Clara's door. "Ah there you are," smiled Clara. "I thought my cooking would bring you home," she chuckled. "Aye, 'tis a grand smell! Would I be right in thinkin' you've been cookin' apples?" "You would be right indeed," grinned Clara. "I've just cored and stuffed four big ones with mincemeat. They should be just about ready by the time we've eaten supper and I'm pretty sure I've got some lovely clotted cream to go with them." "What's for supper?" enquired Jamie. "Beef cobbler," piped Maddy. "I helped Aunt Clara make the dumplings for the top." "Did ye now?" said Tom. "Well, if ya cookin's harf as good as ya Aunt Clara's, we're in fa a real treat." "Why thank you Tom," said Clara, blushing. "I think you'll be impressed, Maddy is a good little cook. Shall we play a game of snakes and ladders while we wait? It's not quite ready," suggested Clara, "Tom and Jamie against Maddy and me." Jamie set the board out on the table. Tom explained that he hadn't played for years and that Jamie would have to remind him of the rules. Within minutes, the game was underway. Tom especially, seemed to be enjoying it. Looking quite chuffed when he threw a six, he looked even more pleased when he and Jamie won the first game. "Shall we make it the best of three?" suggested Clara. "It will give me and Maddy a chance to win one!" They all agreed. Clara and Maddy won the second game. "I think we'll have to play the decider later," said Clara, "as I do believe supper is ready." "Maddy, put the game on the dresser while I serve supper."

Tom's mouth was watering as she placed in front of him, a plate with beef cobbler and dumplings, carrots, Brussels sprouts and peas, all nicely finished off with piping hot new potatoes served with a sprig of fresh garden mint. "Clara you've surpassed ya self," said Tom "'tis a meal fit fa a king." "Tuck in Tom, you don't want it getting cold," said Clara.

The four of them chatted whilst they ate, about the twins going to the local school. Tom told Jamie that he would make new friends, maybe even keep in touch when they went back to the States. Jamie tried to be happy about it, but Tom could sense that although Jamie had no problem staying in England, the thought of having to go to school did not exactly thrill him. Maddy, by total contrast, appeared to quite like the idea. She enjoyed meeting new people and she thought that it would be nice to have a girlfriend to talk to.

Scraping the last spoonful of baked apple from his bowl, Tom stated that he was as full as a pig and that he could not eat another morsel, He joked with Clara that if he kept eating her wonderful home cooking, none of his trousers would fit. Everyone laughed. Clara told him that he worked far too hard to ever put on weight. Maddy and Jamie cleared the dishes while Clara made the tea. She instructed the twins to simply stack the dishes on the drainer and that she would wash them later. Tom passed Jamie the snakes and ladders, to set it up for the deciding game. It was quite a nail biter, with Clara and Maddy winning by a mere two squares.

CHAPTER FIFTEEN

School

Aunt Clara had spoken to the headmaster about the twins going to school. The headmaster was happy about it, although he did think that it would be almost impossible for the twins to be assessed, as the school system in America was fundamentally different. He thought it would be easiest if the twins joined the same class, based on their age. Aunt Clara had agreed.

They arrived at the school just as the bell sounded. They watched as two teachers made the children line up and then in a quiet orderly fashion, instructed the children to enter the school. The twins could feel everyone's eyes on them. Maddy was beginning to think that perhaps school wasn't such a good idea after all. Aunt Clara waited until all the children had entered the school before taking the twins in. First, she took them to the headmaster, Mr. Smith. The twins thought he was very young to be headmaster. Back home, all of the principals seemed to be older. Mr. Smith had only been at the school for two years, but Aunt Clara had been very impressed with him. His own son William attended the school, although he was only six, so he was in the infant section. The ages in the school ranged from five to sixteen, the main reason being that it was the only school for miles around. Many of the children travelled in on the school bus from other villages. Mr. Smith told Clara that he would take the children along to the morning assembly and introduce them to the teachers and pupils. Clara noticed that the twins looked rather nervous at her leaving, so in true Clara fashion, she patted them both on the head and told them that she would be back before they knew it. Taking two neatly packed lunches from her basket, she told Jamie that there was a nice slice of Victoria sponge in there for them.

As Aunt Clara left, Mr. Smith escorted the twins to the assembly hall. Neither of them would have had a clue what assembly was, had Aunt Clara not have explained it to them before. They never had assembly in America; they simply went straight to their class. The assembly hall fell silent as Mr. Smith and the twins entered. The entire senior section of the school was there, ranging in age from eleven to sixteen. The infant section had their own assembly in their part of the school. Maddy could feel the colour rising in her cheeks as Mr. Smith told every one why the twins would be attending the school for a short while and that he would expect everyone to help them find their way around. He introduced them to a young teacher of about twenty, Miss Waller. She was to be their teacher. The twins liked her straight away; she was very friendly towards them. She showed them to two seats, and then rejoined the other teachers. Jamie felt quite relieved as he sat down and glanced over at some of the other teachers. He thought that some of them looked very stern and miserable.

As the assembly finished, Miss Waller took the twins to her classroom. She allocated them a desk next to each other. On Jamie's left there was a ginger haired boy with freckles, who had introduced himself as John Peters. Jamie knew straight away, that he and John would get along fine and as the morning went on Jamie found out that John was quite a character. No less than the class comedian and obviously very popular with Miss Waller. On Maddy's right was a small girl who seemed to look much younger than many of the others. Her name was Dawn Wheeler. Compared to John, Dawn was very shy and quiet, although Maddy thought she seemed very sweet and as usual, Maddy's instincts were correct. By the end of the first day, they had become friends, as did John and Jamie.

Aunt Clara was waiting outside the school gates. "Well? How was your first day?" she asked the twins. "Did you settle in alright? Have you made any new friends?" Maddy was the first to answer. She told Clara all about Dawn and asked if it would be alright if she invited her over for tea after school one day the following week. Aunt Clara was only too pleased for Maddy to bring her friend home. "What about you Jamie?" asked Clara. "Would you like to bring a friend home for tea next week?" He told her about John Peters and that he would like to invite him. Clara frowned.

"I know young Master Peters, is he still playing tricks on people?" Jamie looked surprised, telling Clara that John hadn't done anything bad that day. "Don't you like him?" asked Jamie. "Of course I like him; I've known him since the day he was born. His father is the local vicar, John Senior." "Vicar!" gasped Jamie. "Yes, hard to believe isn't it, what with him being naughty and all. Although in truth, John's not a really bad lad, just a bit loud, probably because he's the vicar's son. He just likes to be the centre of attention." "Has he ever been naughty to you Aunt Clara?" enquired Maddy. "I wouldn't call it naughty as much as I'd say mischievous," replied Clara. "What did he do?" asked Jamie. "Well, back last summer young John and a couple of his friends thought it would be funny to change the colour of my beautiful roses, you know the ones just inside the front gate, the lovely red ones." Maddy looked puzzled. "What did he do?" she asked. "Well, John and his friends sprayed them bright silver." Jamie burst out laughing. "Oh Aunt Clara, what did you do?" "Nothing for a while. I had thought about telling their parents, but decided against it. I waited until I was invited to the vicarage for tea, then I brought up the subject of vandalism. I said that some terrible person had ruined my beautiful roses and should I ever find out who it was, I would have no hesitation in reporting them to the police. Oddly enough, John was unusually quiet throughout tea and each time I glanced over at him he went a deep red colour. He certainly looked very embarrassed and no doubt would think very carefully about doing it again. Despite all that, I would be only too happy for you to invite John over for tea. I'll leave you two to sort it out, just let me know what day you arrange it for, oh and Jamie, don't mention the roses. I wouldn't want the poor lad to feel embarrassed about coming."

Their second day at school was much less stressful than their first. They settled in quickly to their lessons. Miss Waller asked them to tell the class about the schools in America and how the lessons differed from those in England. The twins felt quite important standing in front of the class talking about American school life.

Maddy had taken a dislike to one boy. According to Dawn, he was the class bully, often picking on her because she was shy and not to mention, small. His name was Billy Potter, although behind his back most of the kids nick-named him Billy Big Head. Maddy noticed that he was quite a bit bigger than most of the other boys in the class. In fact, she thought he was fat and after just one day at school, she had noticed how he bullied and intimidated the other boys and some of the girls. He thought it was funny to make them look stupid in front of their friends. Maddy had already decided that she was going to teach Billy a lesson and make him look foolish in front of everybody, but she hadn't quite decided how. She would talk to Aunt Clara about him.

CHAPTER SIXTEEN

The Virus

The twins had now been at the school for two weeks and there was still no clear idea as to when they could return home. The letters they had received from John and Sally had given no indication that the virus was under control, although deaths were now less frequent, due to quick medical treatment. Every day, dozens of new cases were being reported. Judging by the letters, it looked as though the twins could be in England for the foreseeable future and although they were happy to stay with Clara, they were missing their family and friends.

They had both made some really good friends in England and their trips to the fairy village were always fascinating, in fact they had become regular visitors over the weeks. Jamie had become quite a dab hand with weapons and self defence, as had Maddy. Princess Bellaruth had taught her how to fight and use weapons. They had learnt much about the fairy way of life and their history. Princess Michelalena, in particular, was a great story teller, often singing songs about the past. Her voice was like that of an angel. Princess Melissa had helped them to learn more about magic and fairy spells. She was very talented in sorcery and the twins had noticed that, not only could she wrap Wickit around her little finger, but most of the other male fairies too, especially her father, the King. He obviously found it very difficult to say no to Melissa, she just had that certain something about her that allowed her to get away with things.

Nanamic was still concerned about the threat from Stigamites. Although there hadn't been any recent attacks, security at the village was still of paramount importance. She often spoke with Clara about her concerns, convinced that something bad would happen.

Clara and the twins had been invited to the village on Saturday. Apparently, Nanamic and the King had a surprise for the twins. They had repeatedly asked Clara what she thought it could be, and to their disappointment they believed her when she repeatedly told them that she had no idea.

At last Saturday arrived and, as usual, Wickit and Artex arrived to escort them to the village. It was just after seven o'clock in the evening, human time. The journey to the village was normal, no sign of anything sinister lurking in the woods. Once inside the village they were greeted by King Peteron and his family. He told them that he would send for them later, but in the meantime they should enjoy themselves whilst Clara and Nanamic caught up on some gossip.

The twins now knew all the fairies in the village, having been there many times; however, knowing them and remembering all their names was another matter. At night back in the cottage, they would try and remember as many of the names as possible, but no matter how many times they went over them, they always missed some out.

As usual, Jamie went straight to the archery lesson, where his friend Artex was only too pleased to offer him a challenge. Jamie had become very confident, not to mention accurate, with a bow and he was always up for a friendly challenge from Artex. He knew that Artex was by far the best archer in the village and that there was little chance of ever beating him, but knowing this made Jamie try harder. Artex was in no doubt that one day Jamie would actually be able to beat him, a hard enough task for anyone, let alone a human.

Maddy was not really interested in combat; she much preferred to visit the animals with Princess Michelalena. Over the weeks, their friendship had grown stronger. They shared stories about Wobbler and Apple. Maddy had grown very fond of the little fawn, Wobbler, although he was not so little any more. Every time she visited the village, she noticed how much bigger he had grown. The old fairy Link seemed to warm to Maddy. He would often spend time with her and Michelalena. They were fascinated by his stories about the animals he had cared for over the years. Maddy especially enjoyed his stories about unicorns and how no-one had seen one for many centuries, although Link believed, in his heart, that one day unicorns would again take their place amongst us. Maddy hoped that he was right.

As the three friends chatted about Wobbler, a loud bell sounded. It echoed throughout the woods. "What on earth is that!" exclaimed Maddy. Michelalena explained that when the King wanted to summon all the fairies, he would ring that particular bell. As the three of them made their way back to the village, Maddy was bursting with questions about why the bell was ringing and did it have anything to do with the surprise for her and Jamie? Michelalena and Link glanced over at one another and chuckled. Link smiled at Maddy and told her that she asked too many questions and that she and Jamie should feel very honoured that King Peteron and Nanamic felt that they were worthy of a surprise. It was not something that happened very often. As they approached the village, they could see all the fairies congregated in front of King Peteron and Nanamic, who were standing on a small platform. Maddy noticed that her brother was standing in the very front line. The King beckoned to them to join Jamie and Clara at the front. As they took their places next to Jamie and Clara, an eerie silence fell over the crowd. The twins felt slightly nervous, until King Peteron spoke. Firstly, he thanked everyone for coming, and then he asked the twins and Clara to join him and Nanamic. Everyone clapped and cheered. Jamie revelled in it, whereas Maddy felt a bit embarrassed. "I expect you're wondering why we've asked you here today?" asked the King.

CHAPTER SEVENTEEN

The Magic Pearl

Jamie and Maddy sat quietly as the King gave his speech. Even the fairy children listened to his every word. He explained why Nanamic and he felt that something special was in order for the twins. Never before, had two human children, with the exception of Clara and Sally, worked so hard to learn magic and healing potions and, most importantly, learning about the fairies' way of life and culture. He added that with humans like Jamie and Maddy, perhaps one day, fairies and humans would once again be able to live together in peace and harmony.

As the King finished his speech he asked the twins to stand. Nervously they stood before him; even Jamie had butterflies in his stomach. Seeing how anxious they were, King Peteron tried to lighten the proceedings by saying, "Perhaps Clara would like a job teaching all the fairy children the art of magic and healing?" Clara laughed and said that she was far too old to even consider taking on such a huge task. King Peteron told the twins that the gift they were about to receive was only given to a few exceptional individuals and that such a ceremony had not taken place for decades. Jamie and Maddy could barely contain their excitement. Jamie began to fidget. Noticing Jamie's anxiety, the King asked Nanamic to present the twins with their gifts, not wishing to keep them waiting a moment longer. The old fairy, Nanamic, stood in front of the twins. In her hands, she held two tiny boxes. "Step forward Maddy," said Nanamic. The crowd was completely silent as Nanamic passed one of the boxes to Maddy. "Step forward Jamie," she said. As with his sister, she handed him the other tiny box. "Before you open them," said Nanamic, "let me tell you that it is a great honour for me to present you with these gifts. I hope that you will use it wisely and above all, only when it's absolutely necessary." The twins looked baffled. "You may open them now," invited Nanamic. Carefully, the twins opened their boxes. "It's a ring!" gasped Jamie. "Mine too," said Maddy. "Well shall we put them on," said Nanamic, "and make sure they fit?" "Perfect!" said the twins. Maddy admired her ring. It was a pearl held firm in a gold weave, securely mounted onto a gold band. Jamie's was identical. "Oh thank you so much," said Maddy, "it's beautiful." Jamie added, "Yeah, it's well cool!" Everyone laughed, including Nanamic and the King. Jamie could feel himself blushing. "They are no ordinary rings," said the king. "They hold a very special power, which must only ever be called upon in the direst of circumstances and never as a trick, or for fun." The twins could hear the sound of the King's voice become very serious as he spoke to them, but as always, he finished with a smile.

"What do they do? asked Maddy. "Well," answered Nanamic, "they hold the power of invisibility," "What, like you mean we could actually disappear!" "Not exactly disappear; you would still be here but we just wouldn't be able to see you for a short while; you would become invisible." "WICKED!" exclaimed Jamie. Again everyone chuckled at the way Jamie spoke. "How does it work?" asked Maddy. "It's really quite simple. If you look closely enough, you will see a tiny inscription around the gold weave. When you say those words aloud, you will begin to vanish. I suppose a demonstration would be in order to make sure everything is working," said Nanamic, as she looked at the King and smiled. "Oh indeed," replied King Peteron. "Very well then," said Nanamic. "You read your inscription first Maddy." Nervously, Maddy read the tiny words engraved on the ring, and there, before everyone's eyes she began to fade and within seconds, had completely disappeared. Jamie could not believe his eyes. "Maddy," he called, "how is it?" Maddy's voice echoed through the air. "its fine, I don't feel any different. I can still see and hear everything, the same as before. I just can't see myself." "Can I try mine now?" asked Jamie. "Of course," said Nanamic." Just as it had happened with Maddy, as Jamie read the words from his ring, he began to disappear. "It's incredible," said Jamie, "but how do we come back to normal?" "Easy," said Nanamic. "Simply read the inscription backwards, although perhaps I should point out that the magic would only last for a few minutes anyway and you would both be visible again." "That's awesome! Just imagine the tricks we could play on people with these," whooped Jamie. "No Jamie, remember what you have been told," snapped Nanamic. "They are never to be used for fun, only as a last resort when danger is imminent." "Sorry," said Jamie as he reappeared. "I was only kidding." Feeling a little sorry for Nanamic's churlishness, King Peteron stepped forward and in a kindly voice, told Jamie that he didn't think there would be any problem with the twins practising the art of invisibility whilst they were at the village. Nanamic agreed with a cheeky grin. Slowly the fairies went back to what they had been doing before they were summoned to the meeting. Aunt Clara told the twins that they would be leaving shortly, so they were not to venture too far.

CHAPTER EIGHTEEN

Trouble in New York

Back in New York, things appeared to be settling down. The virus was still life threatening, but the scientists had been working around the clock since the outbreak. They had developed an antidote, but it was only successful if it was administered within the first few hours of the illness being diagnosed. After that, it was pure chance whether or not the patient survived, although through good media coverage, more and more people were contacting the hospital at the first sign of the symptoms. "There's a call for you Sally, you can take it at the nurse's station," called Bud. He was one of the orderlies that worked in the emergency department with Sally. Bud was one of Jamie's favourites, always telling him jokes whenever the twins went to the hospital with Sally. Placing the receiver to her ear," Hello! Sally speaking." "OH Sal, it's me, John. Something terrible has happened." Sally could sense the panic in John's voice. "Calm down John, tell me what's happened." "Someone's broken into the house, the police called me about fifteen minutes ago. They want us to meet them there." "Is Debbie okay" asked Sally. "She was there today." "I'm not sure. The police said that there has been some kind of struggle, but no-one was at the house." "What do you mean? Debbie was there, she was helping with the housework!" "I know, I told them that, but they said the house was empty. One of the neighbours called them because they heard shouting and what sounded like glass breaking." Suddenly Sally had an overwhelming fear come over her. Her voice echoed down the phone. "Tell the police that Debbie is still in the house, something's happened to her! exclaimed Sally. "Ok calm down Sal, I'll go and talk to them, but get home as soon as you can."

Immediately after putting down the phone, Sally was heading back home. As she pulled into her street she could see the police car still parked outside. She rushed up to the door where a large policeman was standing. He politely told her that he could not let her in as it was a crime scene. Sally quickly explained that she lived there. As she entered the house, the first thing she noticed was the mess. Judging by the state of the place, every jar, vase and trinket box had been opened and tossed to the floor. Looking through into the lounge, she noticed that John was sitting on the sofa with his arm around Debbie, who was looking very shaken up. Sally noticed straight away that she had bruises and scratches to her face and shoulders. Quickly she rushed over to comfort Debbie. "We would like to ask you a few questions," said a rather stern faced detective. Sally had barely noticed the officers who were standing in the room. She certainly hadn't noticed the forensic team, who were dusting for finger prints. Looking a bit shocked, she apologised to the detective. The first thing he was curious about was the fact that Sally was certain Debbie was still in the house. John had apparently been very persuasive about it, insisting that the officers look again. They were surprised to find Debbie asleep in one of the bedroom closets. At first, they thought she was unconscious or, even worse, dead. They were very curious as to how Sally knew. It was obvious to both Sally and John that the detective was thinking along the lines of an inside job. It wasn't that long before Sally had convinced them that it was purely because she knew that Debbie would not have left, because they were all going to have dinner together, although both Sally and John knew it was nowhere near to the truth. The police asked some more questions; they asked Sally and John to check exactly what was missing and to call the detective with a list. They finally left, after deciding to wait to see what the forensics turned up.

Sally couldn't wait to ask Debbie exactly what had happened. Ironically, Debbie had little recollection of the break in. She could remember hearing something smash upstairs in the twins' room and assumed that something had fallen off a shelf, so she had gone upstairs to investigate. She could remember going into the room, when something grabbed her leg from behind. She thought it was an animal or something like one, because it was definitely small and making strange kinds of growling noises. But for some strange reason, she could not remember what it actually looked like or anything that happened from that point on. John, as always, was looking for the logical answer. "Perhaps it was a raccoon; they can wreak havoc in a house. When I was a boy, we used to vacation at my dad's cabin in the woods. On several occasions 'coons would get in whilst we were out fishing. Mom would go mad when they used to wreck the kitchen. There would be broken china and food everywhere. According to dad, they could pack a nasty bite if you ever cornered one."

Debbie seemed to like John's theory. She was still badly shaken from her ordeal and was glad of any logical explanation, especially as the police didn't seem to have any clues. They had not found any finger prints or anything to help find the culprits.

"Perhaps you should stay here tonight," suggested Sally, "just so I can keep an eye on you." "Thanks Sally, but I'll be fine. I'll stay for a while, maybe I'll remember something. Do raccoons smell John?" "Why?" asked Sally. Debbie sat pondering for a moment. She told them that she remembered smelling something really bad when she went into the twins' rooms, but everything had happened so fast, she had forgotten to mention it. John said that he couldn't be sure, but he would ask his dad. "I'm glad the twins were away," said Debbie,

"God only knows what might have happened." "Well let's put it behind us now," said Sally, "it was probably a one off and John's probably right, it was a raccoon or something." Debbie seemed to take comfort from Sally's words. "Would you like me to take you home?" John asked. "Yes please." "Will you be ok here Sal if I take Debbie home, or do you want to come with us?" "No, I'll be fine."

As soon as they left, Sally headed straight to the twins' rooms; her gut feeling was that there was more to this than anyone first thought. She knew that John's theory on raccoons was probably just a way of making Debbie feel better; after all you don't usually see raccoons in New York. No, Sally had a peculiar feeling that this strange episode had something to do with the twins visit to England, but what?

"Sal, I'm back," called John. "I'm in Maddy's room, come up!"

"Well Sal, what's the damage then?" "Well I'm no detective, but it would appear that who, or what ever it was, they were looking for something." "Looking for what?" "I'm not sure, but I think it may have something to do with the twins' trip to England." "Oh Sal, you're not suggesting that the kids are in some kind of trouble!"

"Good heavens no John, it's just a feeling I've got that's all. I don't think there's anything missing but it's hard to tell. It would seem that something disturbed our intruders. Jamie's room appears to be in the most mess, so I would imagine that was where they started. Come on, I'll show you. I can remember when Clara and I were children, a similar thing happened. I can remember our mother speaking to Nanamic. Trouble is, I don't recall the exact details. It's times like this when I really wish Clara had a phone, because I'm sure she would remember."

"Are you absolutely sure the twins are okay?" "Absolutely! I know that no harm will come to them with Clara and if my suspicions are right, no doubt some one will pay me a visit." "Who will pay you a visit Sal, what do you mean?" "Oh you know John, one of the fairy folk."

"I thought all that hocus pocus was left behind in England Sal." "Oh John, you know it will always be a part of me and the twins, anyway it's a good thing to know that we're protected by fairy magic. Just because I choose not to use it doesn't mean its not there. Anyway, I thought you would be used to it by now." "Correction my darling, I don't think I will ever really get used to it, I've just learnt to live with it. Anyway, would I ever be able to say anything about it? I wouldn't want you turning me into a frog." Sally picked up a pillow from Jamie's bed and hit John with it. "Beware, ribbit ribbit!" she croaked, as they fell onto the bed laughing.

"It's getting late," said Sally. "I'll make some supper then perhaps we should think about turning in. All in all it's been a strange day." John checked that the house was secure, while Sally cleared up the kitchen. "Yep, everything seems okay," said John, "shall we turn in?" "You go ahead, I'm just finishing off and I want to check the twins' rooms." "I checked all the rooms Sal." "Yes I know darling, but I just want to make sure. I'll be along in a few minutes."

Sally sat on Jamie's bed; she seemed to get a stronger feeling in his room. As she sat quietly thinking over the events of the day, she had the feeling that she wasn't alone. Her instincts, as usual, were right. It wasn't long before she found herself in the company of her dear friend Susydix. She was the first fairy Sally had met after moving to the States. Susydix was the American equivalent of Nanamic. She was very highly thought of amongst the fairy folk and none more so than by Nanamic and the King. "I'm glad to see you," said Susydix, "your instincts have not failed you. Today's incident was indeed connected to the twins; I only wish I could tell you why. One thing is for sure, they are doing exceptionally well under Clara's guidance. No doubt you'll be pleased to hear that they are becoming very good in the fairy arts. I know that Nanamic herself is quite amazed at just how quickly they are learning. However, there is definitely something going on in England." "Going on?" queried Sally. "Are the twins alright, is it safe for them?" "Oh for sure," reassured Susydix. "We know that communication is difficult for you, that's why I'm here."

Susydix told Sally about the threat from Stigamites and how this particular group seemed to be different from those the fairies had encountered in the past, far more advanced. "Nanamic has a theory that they have enlisted the help of evil underlords, who in return for certain information, have helped them to move about during the daylight and no doubt increased their powers."

"What do they want?" asked Sally. "Our Oracle is the most logical thought. It heralds great power, which when used correctly, does only good. However, if it fell into evil hands, who knows what might happen." "Oh it sounds terrible, are you sure the twins are ok? Why were we broken into?" Sally's voice sounded shaky. "We think they were trying to take something belonging to the twins, a personal item." "WHY?" "We think it's because the twins pose quite a threat to them. As I said, they have come on so fast and if the Stigamites are planning some type of attack, they want to halt the twins' progress any way they can. If they had been successful in today's raid, they could slow down the twins' learning, but don't worry Sally. As always, your family is protected by fairy magic and we have been watching the house. Nanamic thought that something like this might happen, but rest assured, nothing was taken. We certainly gave them a shock! I'm sorry about your friend though, she was so shaken by the attack, that's why we erased it from her memory. We also treated her with our medicine because she did get scratched, but don't worry she will have no recollection of it. We are watching the house so you shouldn't have any more trouble. You know Sally, we are always there if you need us, you only have to call, oh and tell John I thought his theory about the raccoons was cute. It's just a shame it wasn't; raccoons would be a lot easier to deal with. Talking of John, I would imagine he's wondering where you've got to. Please say hello to him for me, now I really must be going. Take care my friend, we'll speak again soon." Then in a flash of light, Susydix was gone.

CHAPTER NINETEEN

A Lesson for Billy

Things were bustling at Clara's. It was Monday morning and the twins were busy getting ready for school. Jamie was using magic to pack his school bag, because as usual, he had taken too long over breakfast and was subsequently running a bit late. Maddy, as always, was well organized, having packed her bag the night before. She was glad of the extra time. She wanted to talk to Aunt Clara about Billy the school bully and if Aunt Clara thought it would be alright to perhaps use a little discreet magic to bring him down a peg or two. Maddy explained to Aunt Clara how Billy always picked on the smaller kids, even the girls. Maddy did not want to hurt Billy, simply embarrass him.

Clara thought about Maddy's wish to use magic and although it was not really acceptable to use it in public, on this occasion, providing that nobody actually saw Maddy do magic, Clara felt that it would be okay; especially as she had witnessed Billy being a bully when she picked the twins up from school. Maddy was thrilled that she could treat Billy to a taste of his own medicine, although she had not quite decided what she was going to do. She was going to bide her time and decide later on. "See you later," called Clara, as the twins disappeared into the school, "Have a good day."

The twins had settled in really well, they had made some good friends. Dawn and Maddy had become inseparable. They had promised to write to each other when Maddy returned to the States. Maddy had invited Dawn to holiday with them when she was confident enough to fly by herself.

Unlike most of the other kids, Maddy tried not to let Billy get to her, although he was constantly trying to embarrass her about the way she talked and referring to her as the 'cranky Yankee'. She could usually ignore him, only ever answering him back when he tried to bully Dawn. This Monday was the same for Billy as any other day. He was being his usual cocky self, but, unbeknown to Billy, this was not going to be like every other day. No indeed, for this was the day that Maddy would even the score with Billy.

She didn't have to wait long, lunch time in fact. As usual, Dawn and Maddy were sitting on one of the bench tables which the school provided, so that during the nice weather, the children could eat their sandwiches outside. Billy waited until the lunchtime supervisor was talking to a group of children at the other end of the playground, then he walked over to the girls' table and told Dawn to hand over her chocolate bar from her lunch box. Dawn was only too happy to give in to Billy, rather than face a confrontation with him, because like most of them, she was afraid of him. However, on this occasion Maddy was ready for him. Whilst he was busy bullying Dawn, she had quickly and quietly cast a spell over her own lunch box, completely unnoticed by her fellow diners, who were far too busy watching Billy.

"Leave Dawn alone!" said Maddy. "She's not giving you her chocolate bar; you're nothing but a bully!" Billy taunted Maddy by saying that she and Jamie had better watch themselves, or they would be for it. He didn't like Yanks, especially them. In fact, as well as Dawns chocolate bar, he would have Maddy's as well.

"I don't think so," said Maddy in a strong voice. "Oh really?" said Billy, as he snatched her lunch box." We'll see about that!" By now a small crowd had gathered around the table. "Take the lot!" yelled one of Billy's fellow bullies. "Spit in her box!" Maddy made a half hearted grab at getting her box back, not really wanting to succeed. She wanted Billy to open it; she had a surprise waiting for him. Just as she hoped, Billy proceeded to open the box, but nobody was ready for what happened next.

As Billy looked in the box to make his decision as to exactly what he would steal from it, a look of complete horror ravaged his face. He began screaming. "It's a monster, HELP! HELP! It's going to attack me!" A couple of the younger girls started screaming and one started to cry. Billy threw the lunch box into the air. By now he was screaming and sobbing uncontrollably. The lunchtime supervisor had come running over, grabbing hold of Billy, who was, by now, a shaking wreck who could barely talk. "Calm down Billy, calm down!" she ordered. "What on earth is the matter?" Pointing at the box and trying to talk, Billy seemed to be saying that there was a monster in the box that was going to attack him.

"What monster? Where?" said the supervisor. Still trembling in fear, Billy again pointed at the box. "In there! A monster!" At this point Maddy thought it was time to intervene. She stood up and walked over to where her lunchbox had landed. It was lying open, with its contents strewn about on the playground. "There's nothing there Billy," stated Maddy. "But I saw it! There was a huge hairy thing with big fangs!" quivered Billy. Maddy picked the box up, and then with a big grin on her face, she asked Billy if that was the monster he was referring to. Everyone began laughing as they saw the tiny caterpillar that Maddy was pointing to. "It must have crawled in there when we came outside." Billy started ranting about the monster he had seen, although no-one appeared to be taking much notice; they were too busy laughing. Only Maddy knew that Billy was actually telling the truth. For a split second, the tiny caterpillar had indeed been a snarling monster that had filled her lunch box, but it would remain her secret for the time being, at least until she told Jamie and Aunt Clara. She felt that it would be quite a while before Billy took anyone else's lunch. In fact, Billy spent the rest of the afternoon in the sick room; apparently he was feeling unwell. The school nurse thought that perhaps he had had a little too much sun.

CHAPTER TWENTY

Apple

"What a luverly surprise," called Tom, as Clara and the twins pulled into the farmyard. "Sorry to turn up unannounced, but we were at a loose end and didn't have anything to do today, so we thought we would bring our dear friend Tom some home made jam scones," said Clara with a grin.

"You're always welcum here, 'specially when ya bring me scones! I'll put kettle on, so we can 'ave 'em with a nice cuppa tea."

Clara noticed how tidy Tom had tried to keep the farm since they had used magic to help him. "The old place is looking grand Tom; I'd forgotten just how nice it is here."

"Truth is Clara, since ya all 'elped me I've found it a bit easier to do. I 'spose I just needed a bit of a kick start. Trouble is bein' 'ere on me own, thing's can git a bit outa hand 'afore you can turn roun'. Now that you an' the twins pop in, I 'ave a reason to keep it tidy, 'tis a big ole place for just one man though, not sure 'ow much longer I'll be able to do it." "Oh nonsense Tom, you'll never give the farm up!" "Ya prob'ly right, p'raps I should find meself a good woman? Someone like you Clara?"

Clara blushed and quickly asked Tom if it would be okay if the twins went to see Apple. The twins chuckled. They knew that Clara was embarrassed at Tom's suggestion.

In the barn, Maddy called to Apple, who readily appeared in front of her. Hugging him round the neck, she told him that she thought he had grown and that she was so pleased to see that he was still wearing the necklace she had made for him. Raising his head to show off the necklace, it was as though Apple understood what Maddy had said.

Maddy and Jamie had decided that they would teach Apple some tricks. They decided that their first trick would be something simple, like standing on his two hind legs. They were amazed at how quickly Apple picked things up. By the third attempt, he had mastered it. Next, they would try to get him to fetch something for them.

Back in the house, Tom continued to talk about the farm being too big for one person. Clara had always liked Tom; he was a decent, hard working man, but the thought of being romantic with him terrified her. She had never really been into relationships; well not since she had been a young girl. She just thought that she had never met Mister Right. However, she truly valued Tom's friendship and she would never want to do anything to jeopardize it, but there were many times before the twins came to stay when she had felt lonely. Occasionally, if she was honest, she had wished that she had married and had a family of her own. Perhaps she could go out with Tom? She decided to herself that she would wait until he formally asked her out.

"Shall we go and see what the twins are up to?" asked Clara.

"I 'spect they're doin' somethin' with that pig. It's uncanny the way he acts 'round Maddy, 'e's like a dog. Yep, she's definitely got a way with animals Clara, that's fa sure."

Back at the barn the twins were having a whale of a time teaching Apple new tricks. As soon as Tom and Clara appeared, the twins couldn't wait to demonstrate Apple's new talents. Clara and Tom watched as Apple danced on his hind legs, then when Maddy rolled a ball, Apple ran to retrieve it.

"Bravo!" yelled Tom "Tha' woz quite a show, I never realized 'ow clever Apple woz." Maddy asked Clara what she thought.

"Well I never imagined for one minute that you could get a pig to do all that! What's next I wonder, a basket in front of the fire?" Everyone chuckled.

During supper back at the cottage, all they talked about was Apple, except for Maddy telling Clara that she thought Tom was sweet on her. Clara blushed and for the first time ever in front of the twins, found her self a bit tongue-tied. Maddy simply said she thought it was sweet and that they really liked Tom. Clara felt relieved when the conversation stopped suddenly, due to the appearance of Wickit.

"Sorry for the intrusion Clara," said the tiny little man, "but I didn't want to bother you while you were at Tom's, oh and by the way, Maddy is right, Tom is definitely sweet on you Clara!"

"You cheeky little fairy!" said Clara, with a flushed red smile. "Have you been eavesdropping?" "Who me?" chuckled Wickit, "never! Anyway, back to the reason why I'm here. Nanamic would like you to come to the village tomorrow if that's alright? She needs to talk to you about something." "I shall look forward to it, shall we say about three o'clock?" said Clara. "Perfect, I look forward to seeing you all then," replied Wickit and as quickly as he had appeared, he vanished.

"Why do you think Nanamic wants to see you Aunt Clara?" "I really don't know, but for Nanamic to request a meeting is unusual to say the least. Maybe she has some news about America, perhaps they have found a cure for that terrible virus." "That would mean that we would be able to go home," said Jamie. "Yes I suppose it would," replied Clara, with a sad look on her face, "but let's not start guessing and getting ourselves all worked up, after all it could be anything." That night as Clara lay in her bed she couldn't stop wondering about why she had been asked to the village. Her feelings on it however, were that something had happened in America. Sally was on her mind; surely nothing could have happened to her beloved sister? She quickly reassured herself that if something terrible had happened Nanamic would have told her straight away.

CHAPTER TWENTY-ONE

Meeting Susydix

Winston sounded the early morning alarm as usual. Jamie rolled over and tried to ignore him, as he did most mornings. He was just dozing back off to sleep, when a wonderful aroma drifted past him. Aunt Clara was cooking, but this smell wasn't the smell of bacon, no this smell was different, it was sweet. His curiosity got the better of him. Wearily, he made his way downstairs. He hadn't even noticed that Maddy's bed was empty. "What's that smell?" he yawned as he entered the kitchen.

"Ah, good morning Jamie." said Clara. "That smell, my dear boy is coconut. I couldn't sleep, so I decided to get up and make Nanamic some coconut ice. I know she has a very sweet tooth and coconut ice is one of her favourites. Your sister has been helping me. Jamie looked over at his sister and nodded. "What's coconut ice?" "Don't you remember?" asked Maddy. "Aunt Clara used to make it for us when we visited. It's great! We don't have it back home, well not like Aunt Clara's. Look, we've just finished the first batch." Maddy lifted a small tray up.

"Sure, I remember it now," said Jamie, as he looked at the pink and white squares laid out in rows on the tray. "Can I have a bit now?"

"Good heavens Jamie, coconut ice at this hour of the morning!" exclaimed Clara. "Your mother is right; you really do have a cast iron stomach!" The three of them laughed.

"Actually, it's not quite set; it needs to harden a bit. Tell you what, why don't you and Maddy run along and get washed and dressed. I'll set about making us some breakfast, how about scrambled egg?" "Wicked," said Jamie. "I love scrambled egg." "Then perhaps we can have a small piece of coconut ice; it should be just about ready by then." Clara had no sooner made the suggestion than the twins were hurrying off upstairs.

"Coconut ice for breakfast, whatever next," muttered Clara to herself.

"I'll pick you two up early from school today; we mustn't be late for our visit to the village. I suppose a little white lie won't hurt just this once.

"What are you doing today Aunt Clara?" enquired Maddy.

"Oh I've lots of things to be getting on with. Tom is coming over to help me dig the garden ready for my spring bulbs."

Maddy looked at her brother and grinned. "That will be nice for you, just you and Tom."

Clara chuckled; she knew what the twins were implying. "You cheeky pair of scamps! You're worse than your mother; she was always trying to fix me up on dates when we were young. That's where you two get it from." They all laughed.

The morning passed quite quickly. Tom had arrived, as promised, to do the garden. Before they knew it was lunch time. As the two friends chatted over a sandwich and a cuppa, Clara noticed that Tom seemed a bit preoccupied, a bit fidgety. "Is everything alright?" enquired Clara.

"Well, I was wantin' ta ask ya sumthin'. 'Ow do ya fancy cumin' out fa an evenin' with me? P'raps we could go down the pub for sumthin' ta eat? I've 'eard they do a good steak."

"That would be very nice Tom, yes I would love to. You just tell me when." Tom looked relieved. He told Clara that he had been dreading asking her in case she said no.

Clara laughed. "I was a bit nervous myself," she told him. "its many years since I've been out on a date!" The two friends laughed.

Clara told Tom about Nanamic wanting to see her.
"I'm sure 'tis nothin' serious," reassured Tom. "Are the twins goin' with ya?" "Yes of course," replied Clara, "although I do feel a bit wicked Tom. I've had to tell a little white lie about them leaving school early. I told their teacher that they have a dental appointment."

"Oh," said Tom, "that's nothin'. I shouldn't go worryin' yaself about it, that's only a little white lie is that." "Yes I know Tom, but in truth the twins haven't even got a dentist!" The two friends allowed themselves a small chuckle. Half past two arrived. Clara thanked Tom for all his help before waving him off in his truck. "See ya soon," called Tom, as he drove away.

Arriving at the school, Clara could see Miss Waller talking to the twins. It was the mid-afternoon break. All the children were outside playing. Clara walked from her car towards the school gates. Miss Waller spotted her and walked with the twins to meet her.

"Are they just having a check up?! asked Miss Waller in a friendly voice.

"Ah yes, just a check up," answered Clara, hoping that she hadn't blushed too much because she was lying.

Clara thanked Miss Waller then headed back towards the car.

"Oh my word!" stated Clara. "Look at the time, its almost quarter to three. We need to get a move on; we don't want to be late!"

For the first time ever, Clara drove her little car at thirty miles per hour. The twins laughed as Clara told them to hold tight. Their parents always drove at least twice as fast, although the ride in their dad's car always seemed much more comfortable. Poor Aunt Clara's little car was so old even the tiniest bumps in the road seemed huge. Within minutes they were back at the cottage. Clara quickly went inside to fetch the coconut ice she had made for Nanamic.

Thankfully, the walk to the woods was only a short distance and at precisely three o'clock they arrived at the meeting place.

Feeling slightly breathless, Clara expressed her thanks that they had arrived on time and that Wickit wasn't already there.

"I've been here ages," chuckled a familiar voice.

"Wickit!" exclaimed Clara. "I'm so sorry, have you been waiting long?" "Actually," grinned the tiny fairy, "I've only just arrived, I lost track of the time myself." "What were you doing?" enquired Jamie. "Well, it's a secret really," said Wickit. Maddy and Jamie pleaded with Wickit to tell them, promising him that they wouldn't tell anyone.

Clara interrupted. "Its Wickit's business; if he doesn't want to tell you then you really should accept it and leave the poor lad alone."

"Sorry," said the twins. "We didn't mean to go on, Aunt Clara's right, it's your business and if you don't want to tell us, it's okay," said Maddy.

Wickit hung his head down. "It's not that I don't want to tell you, it's just that if the King found out, there would be severe consequences."

"We promise we won't tell anyone," said Jamie. Although he was bursting with anticipation and he really wanted to know, he knew that he shouldn't really force Wickit into telling him.

Clara sensed a kind of sadness in the young Wickit.

"Is everything alright Wickit? I'm sure that whatever it is, nothing's as bad as it may seem." Clara spoke in a caring manner. Wickit felt reassured by Clara's kindness. He knew that she, of all humans, could be trusted implicitly. "Oh Clara," said Wickit, "if only this were true, then my heart would not feel so heavy." Clara held out her hand for the tiny fairy to stand on. "What is troubling you, my dear Wickit?"

"Well, it's the Princess Mel...; Wickit hesitated for a moment, Melissa. We love each other so much, but the King will never allow us to marry."

Clara looked at him. "I know," she said, "although I believe there have been occasions when such unions have been permitted. I also know that King Peteron thinks very highly of you. If fairy law allowed it, he would welcome you as a husband for Melissa, as would his entire family."

"This would be true," said Wickit. "It's a hopeless situation Clara. We've spoken about it to Melissa's Aunt Helena." "Who's that?" piped Jamie. "Helena is the King's sister, she's Melissa's favourite aunt. She is very kind, especially to Melissa. I'm sure you two will meet her today, she's back at the village for a while." "Doesn't she live there all the time?" enquired Maddy. "She is our envoy; she travels around all the fairy villages, discussing important matters. Had the queen still been alive, I doubt Helena would have taken the position." "Why not?" "Well you see, they were very close. When the queen was killed she was devastated. We all believe that's why she took the position. Even she doesn't think there's a way of getting round it. Fairy law is fairy law. We have decided that if we have to keep our love secret to all but a few, then so be it. I would rather die than be apart from her. We have loved each other since we were children. I would gladly give my own life for Melissa. Sorry Clara, we will have to continue this conversation later, they will be expecting us at the village and Nanamic doesn't like anyone to be late." "That's for sure," chuckled Clara.

No sooner had they spoken when the forest appeared to light up and just as before, the fairy village came into view. Within seconds Princess Melissa was flying towards them. "Hello," she called, as she landed next to Wickit, grabbing hold of him to steady herself. "Steady," chuckled Wickit, "you'll have us both over."

"Hello there Clara," called a voice that she recognised immediately as the King's. "Nanamic is looking forward to seeing you, something about coconut ice I believe" muttered the King.

"How does she know we've made coconut ice?" questioned Jamie. "Allow me to answer," said the king. "It's a gift that Nanamic seems to have. She always seems to know what Clara will bring. Many times I've asked her, as always she never tells me. Queen Kaznia always told me that Nanamic had spies everywhere. Unfortunately, I've never been able to prove it," he turned to Wickit, "have I?" he said with a grin.

King Peteron told the twins to go and find the others while Aunt Clara spoke to Nanamic. Just as the twins were about to go, the king told them that he had heard a lot about the piglet Apple and how talented he was. Jamie and his sister were quite shocked when he said that, on their next visit, they could bring Apple with them and that Link and the children would love to meet him.

Clara handed Nanamic the coconut ice. As she did, she was sure the old fairy's eyes actually sparkled. "I believe you've been expecting this," she said, smiling. Opening the wrapping, Nanamic could not resist breaking off a small corner and popping it into her mouth. Still chewing her coconut ice, she asked Clara if she remembered Susydix. "Of course," replied Clara, "how is she?" "Oh she's fine, although you can ask her yourself. She will be joining us any moment." No sooner had she spoken when Susydix arrived. "Hello Clara, how "wonderful to see you again, how are you?" "I'm well thank you."

"No doubt you've had your work cut out for you, looking after the twins all these weeks." "Oh it's been wonderful," said Clara, "I shall really miss them when they go back to the States." "I suspect that won't be long. Things seem to be calming down in regard to this awful virus. In fact, I spoke to Sally just two days ago. It would appear that the scientists have now found a cure. They're simply being cautious before they give the all-clear." "How are Sally and John?" asked Clara. "They are well Clara, although I think John is still a bit shaken from the break-in." "Break in!" exclaimed Clara. "Are they alright?" "Yes, they're fine. It wasn't a break in the traditional sense; it was more that someone was looking for something specific. "Whatever do you mean?" asked a rather confused Clara. Nanamic interrupted. "This is why Susydix is here, Clara, to explain to you first hand exactly what has been going on in America."

Susydix told Clara about the Stigamite attack at Sally's house, explaining that they were probably looking for a personal item belonging to the twins. "Why?" enquired Clara. "It's quite simple really," replied Susydix. "If they use black magic on the item, they can cause havoc for its owner. "Good heavens!" exclaimed Clara."They didn't get anything, did they?" "Absolutely not! We had expected this sort of thing to happen, so we had the family under the watchful eye of our very best warriors, as the Stigamites found out to their absolute horror." "May I just say, Clara," said Nanamic, "you know that I trust Susydix with my own life, which is precisely why I asked her to watch over your family."

"Please may I ask why they would want to hurt the twins?" asked a rather confused Clara. "Surely they cannot see them as a serious threat?" "On their own, they would not pose much of a threat, but combined with others such as you Clara, they could be. They have certainly picked things up quicker than any other humans we've ever come across. They are definitely a force when they're together. Our elders believe it may be because they're twins. When their powers are used together, they are as strong as any warrior of the fairy realm." "Correct me if I'm wrong Nanamic, but I thought the Stigamites had all but disappeared," said Clara. Nanamic paused before answering.

"You are partly correct Clara, they have all but disappeared. However, we believe they are in league with the Bawllows. Despite our best efforts, we are at a loss to know exactly what is going on, which makes us a bit vulnerable, although we are prepared for anything and we could be worrying for nothing. It may not be us they intending to attack." "Who then?" asked Clara. "It saddens me to tell you Clara, that an entire elfin colony has been destroyed. Every elf was killed, except for a few children who were taken. All our efforts to find them have proved futile."

"Are you sure it was Bawllows?" "Absolutely! The way in which the elves were slaughtered can only mean Bawllows. What is most worrying is the fact that we believe the Stigamites have joined with them. We always believed that they feared them as we do. Dragonscott is no fool; he knows how dangerous Stigamites are. We can only imagine they have struck some kind of a bargain.

Still that's enough talk about horrible things, how are things between you and Tom?" Clara could feel herself blushing as she struggled to answer. "Ah yes," interrupted Susydix, "I hear from Nanamic that things are warming up in the romance department, good on ya Clara, it's about time." Clara, for once, was lost for words. She barely managed to say that she was simply going out for dinner with him. Nanamic could see Clara was struggling and typically she wanted to help, so she simply said that everyone held Tom in very high regard and should Clara ever decide to become romantically involved with Tom she would, without a doubt, have the blessing of everyone in the village. Clara thanked her. "Now shall we take Susydix to meet those twins we talked so much about? I believe Helena is also keen to meet them, so we shall make it a double introduction." Jamie and Maddy told Helena and Susydix all about Apple and that King Peteron had invited Apple to the village. They chatted for ages, leaving nothing out, not even the fact that Tom was sweet on Aunt Clara. Obviously the two fairies knew about everything the twins were saying; however, with true fairy politeness, they behaved not only as if they were interested, but also surprised, just as Nanamic did every time Clara brought her a present. As they walked back to the cottage under the watchful eyes of Wickit and Artex, the twins told Aunt Clara how much they had liked Helena and Susydix, adding that Susydix was quite plump for a fairy. Wickit and Artex laughed.

CHAPTER TWENTY-TWO
Apple's Big Day

School kept the twins busy, which helped the week pass more quickly. Tom seemed to keep Clara busy with endless offers of gardening and so forth. Maddy couldn't wait to see Apple, she hoped that the now not so little piglet would remember the tricks she had taught him. Aunt Clara had reassured her that she had no doubts about it. Finally, the day of the visit to the fairy village arrived. As arranged, Tom had arrived early to bring Apple over for his big debut. He had taken the time to give Apple a bath and he had polished the tiny ball which hung around his neck.

"Oh you look so handsome!" exclaimed Maddy, as she greeted Tom and Apple. "I presume ya talkin' to the pig," chuckled Tom.

Something felt strange to Jamie as they walked to the village; Aunt Clara had also felt it. "Stay close," she called to Maddy, who was in front with Apple and totally oblivious to the strange feelings of her companions. "I'll be leavin' ya now," said Tom. "I believe ya escort is 'ere." Wickit appeared from behind a bush. "Well spotted Tom," he said, "I was going to surprise you all." "Make us jump you mean," stated Clara drily. "Ah well yes, something like that," chuckled Wickit.

Once Tom was out of sight they entered the village. All the children were excited to meet Apple. He performed wonderfully for them just as Aunt Clara had predicted. Even King Peteron and Prince Iandrew seemed amused. Clara, as usual, was inside drinking tea with Nanamic. Everything seemed normal at the village except for one thing. The twins noticed that Artex and some of the other warriors were absent. Jamie was just about to ask Maddy where she thought they might be, when suddenly a loud bell rang out through the village.

All at once everyone started running and shouting, it was obvious that something terrible was about to happen. Instinctively the twins, along with Apple, ran towards Nanamic's house. Suddenly, they felt themselves being lifted into the air. Looking up, they saw King Peteron and Prince Iandrew carrying them to towards Nanamic's. As they flew over the village, they saw Princess Michelalena taking all the children into the school. They were horrified by what they saw happening below them. The ugly twisted figures of Stigamites and Bawllows battled with the fairy warriors. Without warning, Maddy felt herself falling. Prince Iandrew had been hit in the arm by a stray arrow! "GOT YOU!" came the familiar voice of Princess Bellaruth as she caught Maddy in mid air. Gently, the King and Bellaruth put the twins down at Nanamic's door and Aunt Clara quickly took them inside.

As they watched from Nanamic's window, they saw creatures even more grotesque than Bawllows attacking the fairies; their huge claws and fangs ripping into their flesh, they were relentless. Maddy's heart was pounding as two of the creatures rushed towards the house. "THEY'RE COMING, THEY'RE COMING!" she screamed. Nanamic threw a ball of fire at them, but still they kept coming. "It's me they're after," she gasped, "they want our Oracle, you must help us Clara!" she exclaimed. "Of course we will," said Clara, "just tell us what to do!" "You must take the Oracle! Whatever happens, they must not get it, no matter what!" cried Nanamic. "I will lead them away from here. With the help of your invisibility spell, you can take the Oracle to safety; our whole future depends on you!"

No sooner had she spoken than she flew out of the door and up into the evening sky, pursued by the two Bawllows. Clara and the twins could hear her voice on the breeze, telling them to run and hide. "Quickly children use your rings to disappear!" said Clara. "Give me the Oracle," said Jamie. "I will find Artex and the others, they will protect us." Having no time to argue, Clara passed the Oracle to Jamie. "Now hurry you two!" "Aren't you coming with us Aunt Clara?" "No my dear, I'm far too slow. I'll hide here. Now that Nanamic has gone, they may not come back for a while."

As ordered, the twins made themselves invisible and carefully, they tried to make their way to the forest. Suddenly, they found themselves in the midst of a fight between Artex, Wickit and several Bawllows. The most grotesque was Dragonscott. They knew it was him, even though he was in his true form. He was taunting Wickit by telling him that his reward for helping the Stigamites was to be the Princess Melissa. Despite being outnumbered, Wickit fought like a true warrior. "I must help them," cried Jamie, as he passed the Oracle to Maddy. "No!" cried Maddy. "We must hide, remember what Nanamic said, we must save the Oracle!" "Then do it," shouted Jamie. "I must fight!"

Still invisible, he picked up a sword lying on the ground next to the body of a fairy warrior and without the slightest hesitation, he lunged it into the back of a Stigamite. At that precise moment he started to become visible, the spell was wearing off. "Glad to have you with us!" called Artex. The three friends fought gallantly, even the mighty Dragonscott was seriously wounded. Wickit flew over Jamie and cast a fairy spell, 'FAIRY GOODNESS, FAIRY LIGHT, GIVE THIS WARRIOR THE POWER OF FLIGHT.' He sprinkled dust from his wings down onto Jamie. Suddenly, Jamie was rising into the air. "Follow us!" called Wickit. "We must protect the school, the Princesses Michelalena and Melissa are there with the children."

Within seconds they were outside the school fighting more grotesque creatures. Meanwhile, on the ground, Maddy, who by now was also visible, was still running towards the forest. Suddenly, without any warning, a huge grotesque creature was standing in front of her, fresh blood still dripping from its distorted mouth and razor sharp fangs. Momentarily frozen by fear, Maddy fumbled with her invisibility ring, trying to grip the Oracle as tightly as she could. Aware that the creature had seen it, she tried desperately to recite the spell, the creature moving closer with every passing second. Suddenly, as the beast swiped his huge clawed hand directly at her, he seemed to lose his balance, falling backwards and hitting the ground with a heavy bone-crushing thud. Not understanding her good fortune

Maddy, looked down at the creature, which appeared to be coming round. Stunned, she noticed something moving from underneath the creature's legs. It was Apple! He was obviously responsible for the creature's condition, having rammed it from behind and sending it off balance. Bending down to cuddle Apple, she had an idea, which would later prove to be the best she ever had.

She led Apple to where she knew Link would be with his animals. She knew he would protect them at all costs. Once she found Link, she told him to watch over Apple for her until she returned to collect him. Link pleaded for her to stay with him, but she insisted that she must find her brother and Aunt Clara.

Returning to the thick of the battle, she saw many fairies slain, along with many Stigamites and Bawllows. She had made herself invisible again so she was able to move about with relative ease. In the distance, she could see Jamie still fighting alongside Artex and Wickit. She felt a strange sense of pride in the way her brother fought. Returning to Nanamic's, she found Aunt Clara, who appeared to be stuffing tiny balls into her pockets, assisted by Nanamic, who had managed to give her pursuers the slip. "What are you doing?" asked Maddy. "Oh thank goodness you're alright my dear, I was so worried about you!" exclaimed Clara with a look of relief. "Where's Jamie?" Maddy explained what had happened. "We must find him," wailed Clara. "If anything happens to him I just don't know what I will do." "He's still at the school, I saw him on my way here." "Then we must not waste any more time!" exclaimed Nanamic.

They made their way towards the school. Nanamic said to Clara that things did not look good, the fairies appeared to be losing their gallant battle, there were simply too many Stigamites and Bawllows. Suddenly they were surrounded. Nanamic flew high into the air chanting a spell as she rose. Clara reached into her pocket. Grabbing a handful of the small balls, she threw them at the enemy. Above them Nanamic continued with her spell, dodging balls of fire as she went. As the balls Clara had thrown hit the ground, fiery explosions erupted, followed by a dense fog. Momentarily they were hidden from their enemy. At that precise moment Nanamic finished her spell, sprinkling fairy dust down onto her friends. "You will be invisible for a short while," she called. "Find somewhere to hide, I must find King Peteron and the others. Fairy speed be with you!" she called as she disappeared from sight. "Quickly!" said Clara, "we must hide before the spell wears off." Maddy led Clara to Link, hoping that they could hide with him in the forest.

Back at the village, Nanamic searched frantically for her family, grief stricken by what she saw, so many fairies wounded or killed. At last she found them. All that were left able to fight were defending the school. King Peteron had been wounded; a huge gash could be seen through his tunic. Despite this, he continued to fight to defend his people to the very last breath if need be. Calling to Nanamic he yelled, "We must save the children!" He implored her to take them to the forest via the secret passage under the school. "Take Bellaruth with you," he called. Upon hearing this, Princess Bellaruth shouted, "No way father, I will stay and fight!" Knowing that she was as good as any warrior and that she was mutinously stubborn, the King told Nanamic to go without Bellaruth.

Princesses Michelalena and Melissa were trying to keep the children calm; they both welcomed Nanamic's arrival. Quickly they made their way through the secret passage and to the relative safety of the forest. "I must return to help your father and the others," said Nanamic. The princesses knew that any pleading to make her stay would be futile. "Take care!" they called as she left.

As she approached the school, Nanamic was heart sore, she could see many more warriors had fallen. King Peteron was barely able to wield his sword, he was growing weaker. Just as all hope appeared to be lost, a strange noise carried on the wind; it was the sound of the elves' horn! Nanamic could see through the smoke and dust. Mina, Queen of the Elves was leading her warriors towards the battle, charging at all who stood in their way. Overwhelmed, the Stigamites and Bawllows took to their heels and fled back to the dark murky depths of the earth. A loud cheer went up all around the village. The wounded were being helped to their feet, many were crying over the loss of their loved ones who had fallen.

Nanamic and the King greeted Mina warmly, expressing their gratitude for her help. Mina spoke on behalf of her people, stating that for too long, there had been ill will between the elves and the fairies; it was time to put to rest all their differences and unite in the common cause. Nanamic and the King agreed. Calm was slowly restored to the village; the wounded were treated and many bodies were laid to rest. Although with the elves help they had won a victory, the price they had paid was high.

As the last elves left, Nanamic told King Peteron that she feared that worse was yet to come and that she feared the Oracle had fallen into the hands of the Bawllows, or even worse, the Stigamites. Rising quickly to his feet, the King summoned every warrior who was able to fly or walk. "Our Oracle has been taken!" he shouted. "We must find it before it's too late!" Still very weak from his injuries, King Peteron held his sword in the air to signal to the warriors to move. "WAIT, WAIT!" shouted a familiar voice. Straining his eyes to peer through the smoke, King Peteron spotted Maddy with Apple. She was waving frantically. "We must hurry," said King Peteron, looking down on the small human girl who was trying very hard to catch her breath. Nanamic stepped forward. Placing her hand on Maddy's shoulder, she asked what was so important that it couldn't wait. Regaining her composure, Maddy blurted out, with a wheeze, that she had the Oracle. Nanamic looked Maddy up and down, hoping to see it. "Where is it?" she asked. "I don't have it on me at the moment," replied Maddy. With panic in her voice, Nanamic asked if she knew where it was. "Yes, of course," replied Maddy, "it's right here!" pointing at Apple. "What are you telling us?" questioned Nanamic, "that the pig has it, or knows of its whereabouts?" Kneeling down beside Apple, Maddy undid the tiny necklace she had made for him, gently patting the young pig on the head before standing up. She then proceeded to unscrew the tiny ball which hung from it, gently tapping the contents into the palm of her hand. "Here it is," she said holding out her hand to show Nanamic. The elderly fairy squinted to see exactly what it was that Maddy was showing her. Realizing that Nanamic had very poor eyesight, Maddy quickly began to chant a spell. Lo and behold, before their very eyes, the tiny object in her hand began to grow. Within seconds, everyone recognized it as their Oracle. Embracing Maddy in her arms, Nanamic told her that she had saved the day. A mighty cheer rang out through the village. When all the excitement had calmed down, Maddy explained that she had the idea to use Apple in the hope that neither the Stigamites nor the Bawllows would imagine for one minute, that a pig could have the Oracle. "She's a very smart witch, that niece of yours Clara," added the King, "very smart indeed!"

CHAPTER TWENTY-THREE

The Wish

King Peteron called a meeting of the elders. It was decided that, because of their bravery, together with Maddy's cunning plan to save the Oracle, the twins should be rewarded. Never before had such an honour been given to any human. However, on this occasion, it was unanimous, every elder agreed. Nanamic thought that a single wish should be granted to the twins. The elders agreed. This was indeed a wonderful offer; the rewards of such a wish could be unending. So it was decided; a single wish they would get.

Maddy, Jamie and Clara were invited to the King's palace. Even Aunt Clara was nervous. She had never seen inside it, although it was everything she had ever imagined. Magnificent in every detail, from the fine furnishings, to the spun silk rugs that covered the walls and floors.

King Peteron apologized for keeping them so long, knowing that they probably wanted to return to their cottage after the momentous events of the day. "Oh that's okay," piped Jamie, "it was worth staying to see your home!" King Peteron grinned at Clara. He explained that they were the only humans ever to go inside his palace, adding that if he had more time and had the palace not have been damaged during the battle, he would have been only too pleased to have shown them around. However, his only concern at the present time was to tell them what Nanamic had proposed as a special reward.

As always Jamie was the first to speak up, "What! You mean we can wish for anything we want?" King Peteron nodded, then explained that it was only one wish between them and they should decide carefully, not to mention wisely. They would have precisely one week in which to decide. After that, the wish would be forfeited. Clara and the twins thanked the King and Nanamic, then, under the ever watchful eyes of Wickit and Artex, they returned to their cottage.

"What a day!" sighed Clara, as she slumped into her chair. "Who would have thought when we left earlier, that we would be in the thick of a battle and that a little pet pig called Apple would save the day? I can only try and imagine what Tom will think when Wickit returns Apple to him later. I'm sure Tom will be amused to think that his pig played the most important part of the day.""Did you see me fighting Aunt Clara?" boasted Jamie. "Was I great or what?""Oh absolutely," replied Clara, "although I must say young Jamie, your sister's ingenious plan to hide the Oracle was equally as daring. I only hope the village can recover from these terrible events, although I'm sure King Peteron will soon have things back to normal. It's so sad for the fairies that lost kin folk. It will be a long time before they recover from that. Despite all the sadness of today, things could have been a lot worse, heaven only knows what would have happened if the Oracle had fallen into enemy hands. The consequences don't bear thinking about. Perhaps we should have supper, followed by an early night. I'm sure we'll all feel better after food and a good night's sleep. Then first thing tomorrow morning, we can decide what to do with your wish."

CHAPTER TWENTY-FOUR

A Dream Come True

"Come on you two," called Clara up the stairs. "If you don't soon get up, half the day will be gone." Maddy mustered from her sleep; slowly her eyes began to focus. Looking round the bedroom, she could see that Jamie was dead to the world. "Jamie wake up, Aunt Clara is calling us!" "Uhh," came the reply. "We've got to get up, she's cooked breakfast." Jamie stirred. Breakfast! "Why didn't you wake me?" "Oh come on," said Maddy crossly. As usual, Jamie was first to the table. "Smells great Aunt Clara! I'm starving," he added. Clara laughed. "I expect you are, after yesterday's adventure." Jamie ate his way through sausage, bacon, eggs and toast, stating that he was too full to move. "Oh no," exclaimed Maddy, "look at the time! We're going to be late for school." "Don't panic my dear," reassured Aunt Clara, "school has been cancelled today." "What do you mean?" asked Jamie. "Well my dears, at about a quarter to seven, Mr. Jenkins, the school caretaker, dropped a note through my door. Certain parts of the school were flooded due to a burst water pipe. Apparently, it has been pouring out all over the weekend, he's hoping that a plumber can sort it out today. That's why I let you two have a lie in this morning. I think you might have slept all day Jamie, even trusty old Winston couldn't stir you this morning."

"What are we going to do today?" asked Maddy. "Well, I think we really should discuss your wish." "Oh that's easy," piped Jamie, "there's a really cool mountain bike I want." "Hang on a minute there bro, who said you could pick?" snapped Maddy. Anyway, it was my idea to hide the Oracle and I want a pony!"

"Oh yeah Maddy. I'm sure mum and dad will go for that, you wouldn't be able to keep it in New York."

"Actually Jamie, I was going to ask Tom if he would look after it for me." Before Jamie could answer Maddy back, Aunt Clara intervened. "Now now you two! That's enough!" The twins noticed a stern tone in Aunt Clara's voice. "This is precisely why I suggested discussing the issue. It's a very serious decision, not something to be taken lightly; the consequences of a bad choice could have terrible repercussions." Maddy looked at her brother. "Aunt Clara's right Jamie, we need to think very carefully about it." Clara nodded her approval at Maddy's show of maturity. "What do you think we should wish for Aunt Clara?" asked Jamie.

"Oh heavens above, now there's a question!" she replied. "I suppose if I were younger, I could think of a thousand things. However, at my age, there really aren't that many things I need. I suppose I've always been happy with my lot. If I'm honest, I would probably try to help others with it, but it's your wish, so it must be your decision. Perhaps it would be best if we forgot about it for today and went to visit Tom. I'll take him some marmalade; I made a batch last week. What do you to think of that idea?" The twins smiled and nodded in agreement.

They had a great time at Tom's, the main topic of conversation being Apple. Tom seemed quite proud that his little pig had saved the day. As a special treat he had given Apple a cheese sandwich, not a usual pig snack, but certainly one of Apple's favourites. As always, Clara invited Tom back for lunch. He declined her offer, although he did suggest going out for their meal at the end of the week. Maddy nudged Jamie while they waited for Clara to reply. They grinned when she said yes!

They teased Aunt Clara all the way back to the cottage about her date with Tom, although she insisted that they were just good friends, who were going out for a meal together. Clara was quite relieved to get back inside her cottage and start preparing lunch, happy to send the twins outside to play and get a minute's peace and quiet.

During lunch, Maddy told them that she had an idea about what to wish for, Jamie looked curious. Clara asked her what her idea was. "Well, I've been thinking about it while we were at Tom's farm. What you said this morning Aunt Clara, made me realize how lucky we are. We have everything we need, plus fairy magic to protect us. What more could we possibly want? I would really love a pony but that wouldn't be fair to Jamie 'cos he really wants a mountain bike." Unable to contain himself Jamie told Maddy to get to the point! Maddy looked at Clara. "I'm not even sure if what I'm thinking is even possible, but I think you might know Aunt Clara." "What is it dear?" said Clara. "Does fairy law allow fairies to be included in a wish?" Clara thought about it for a moment. "Well, King Peteron did say it was your wish and that anything was feasible. He certainly didn't say it couldn't be for one of his people, although realistically, I suppose it would depend on what it was."

Jamie, by this point, was fit to burst! "Oh come on Maddy, what is it?" Maddy frowned at him, then stated that he was just like their dad, no patience whatsoever! Clara couldn't help but giggle to herself, Sally was always moaning about John's lack of patience.

"I've been thinking how nice it would be to help Wickit. We both know how much he loves Princess Melissa. It's so sad that they will never be able to marry because of some stupid fairy law. I just thought it would be wonderful if we asked King Peteron if it would be alright to wish that Wickit could marry Melissa."

"You're such a thoughtful girl Maddy, I'm so proud to be your aunt," stated a rather overwhelmed Clara. "Your mum always tells me how kind and sensitive you are. If you want my opinion, I think it's a truly wonderful idea, but of course, Jamie would have to agree." They waited for Jamie to answer, secretly both thinking that he would want to use the wish for something else.

Jamie looked a bit deflated and did not want to be outdone by Maddy. He could see that Aunt Clara was brimming with pride and thought it a great idea, so Jamie simply looked at them and said, "Yeah okay, seems like a good idea. On one condition Maddy; you try and talk dad into getting me a mountain bike for Christmas." "Sure thing!" replied his sister.

At that moment, a slight pang of guilt rippled through Clara. Did the twins really understand the true magnitude of such a wish? Most people would give their back teeth to have the offer of anything they desired. Would Sally and John have been so willing for them to give away a chance of a lifetime? In her wisdom, she decided to go over the consequences of such an important decision. Then, and only then, would she be comfortable with whatever they agreed on. After an hour and a half of discussion, Clara asked the twins if they still wanted to give their wish up for Wickit and Melissa. Offering to make some tea, she left the twins alone to decide. Fifteen minutes later she returned with a fresh pot of tea and three large slices of lemon cake. Passing the cups over, she asked if they had decided.

Without hesitation, Maddy told Aunt Clara that they wanted to give the wish to Wickit and Melissa, if the King would allow it.

"What was that?" Jamie spun round in his chair. He had heard something behind him. Quietly, the trio watched. "It came from the dresser," said Jamie, "I definitely heard something.""You can come out now! said Clara. The twins just looked at each other.

"Come on, out you come!" Wickit stepped gingerly out from behind a china plate. "How long have you been eavesdropping?" asked Clara? Looking very guilty Wickit tried to tell her that he had only just arrived! It was obvious by the look on Clara's face that she didn't believe him, but for whatever reason she didn't make an issue of it. She simply asked him why he had come. "Nanamic sent me, to tell you that many of the warriors who were injured will make a full recovery. Also, that the village is already returning to near normal. Finally, she said to tell you that we are truly in your debt. If there's ever anything she can do for you, all you need to do is ask."Clara thanked him and told him to tell Nanamic how glad she was to hear that things were okay. Also of the utmost importance, was that Maddy and Jamie had decided what they wanted for their wish. Wickit wished then all a good afternoon and then in a flash, he disappeared. "Do you think he heard us Aunt Clara?" "Oh for sure, Wickit is far too nosey. If he didn't already know, he would most certainly have asked," replied Clara. "Will he tell the king?" "Not if he knows what's good for him; he knows King Peteron would be very angry with him for eavesdropping."

CHAPTER TWENTY-FIVE

The Wedding

Finally, the day arrived to return to the village. As they entered with Wickit, they were surprised how normal everything looked. Nobody would ever have thought that a terrible battle had taken place there just a few days earlier. Even the school had been repaired. The mushroom shaped roof had been re-thatched; shoots from new plants were springing up all around the village.

King Peteron and Nanamic were waiting as Clara and the twins walked into the village. "Welcome," said King Peteron. All the fairies gathered round in total silence while the king spoke. Placing his hand on Clara's shoulder, he told her that a great debt was owed to her and the twins, adding that he was humbled in their presence. Clara was speechless. Continuing, King Peteron asked if they had come to a decision, one that they were all in agreement with. Clara nodded. "Then we shall proceed. Who wishes to tell me what you have chosen?" Clara nominated Maddy, as the original decision had been hers. "Very well," said the King. "Maddy, what is your wish?"

Feeling rather nervous at this point, Maddy took a deep breath, and then proceeded to tell him that they would like Wickit to be able to marry the Princess Melissa. A hush echoed through the crowd. Nanamic stepped forward. "Is your brother absolutely sure this is what he wants?" "Yes," replied Maddy. Jamie nodded his head. "Then I feel we should consider granting your wish, don't you?" she said, looking at the King. "After all, you did say they could have any wish they chose."

King Peteron was momentarily lost for words; never in a million years did he ever imagine two human children wishing for such a thing. Regaining his composure, although still looking slightly baffled, he agreed with Nanamic, that a promise was indeed a promise and that any good king should grant such a wish. Tension in the crowd was mounting. Wickit and Melissa stood like frozen statues. Raising his hand in true leader fashion, King Peteron clearly spoke the words, "THEN SO BE IT."

Everyone began cheering and clapping. Melissa threw herself into her father's arms and thanked him, and then she kissed his cheek. With tears in her eyes she told him that she was the happiest princess in the Kingdom. Looking down on his beloved daughter, Peteron told her to go over to her husband to be, because he looked pale and his knees appeared to be knocking together. The crowd roared with laughter, even Nanamic and Clara. Moments later, the King raised his hand to order silence. Looking at Maddy and Jamie, he told everyone to remember this day as it was a day when others put the happiness of two individuals before their own. Then he bent down and kissed Maddy's hand, before shaking Jamie's. He had foreseen that the twins would be returning home very soon, so he spoke to Nanamic about arranging the wedding before they went, adding with a laugh, that it would be a very short engagement! Thanking everyone for their time, the King turned to walk away. He was stopped by Maddy's voice calling him back. "Yes Maddy," he asked, "did you want to ask me something?" "Please Your Majesty," replied Maddy, raising her head up as if to whisper something to him. She asked very quietly, "Can Tom come to the wedding? Only he's dating Aunt Clara. She won't admit it, but she's really sweet on him." Standing up straight before answering her, he informed the crowd that Tom, the owner of Apple, would be invited to the Royal wedding. Everyone cheered. Aunt Clara looked completely baffled. When they returned to their cottage Clara asked Maddy what she had said to the King. "Simple," she replied. "I just told him that you and Tom were dating!" For the second time in one day, Aunt Clara was speechless!

CHAPTER TWENTY-SIX
Gifts for the Twins

As predicted by the King the telegram arrived two days later from Sally to say that the twins could return home at the end of the month. On the very same day an invitation to the Royal wedding was given to them by Wickit, it read.

'You are ordered to attend the wedding of Princess Melissa to Prince Wickit.' "Oh so you're a prince now! said Clara. With a huge grin on his face, Wickit replied "Indeedy!" Looking rather pleased with his new Royal title, he explained that Princess Melissa would never be allowed to marry a commoner. Hence the king saw fit to honour him with the title. Wickit told them that had it not have been for their wish, he would probably never have been able to marry the love of his life, Melissa. He added that if, at any time in the future, they could be of any help to Clara or the twins, they would be only to happy to oblige. Also, when they have a family of their own they would name them Jamie and Maddy, in honour of the twins! "Good heavens!" said Aunt Clara. "Surely one Jamie is enough!" They all laughed.

"I must go now," said Wickit. "Nanamic and Melissa want to go over the wedding plans, and woe betide me if I'm late!" chuckled the tiny man. Then as always, there was a flash and Wickit was gone. Another flash and he was back. "Almost forgot, Melissa told me to instruct you all to visit Tom today!"

Worried as to why, Clara asked if Tom was alright? "Absolutely!" replied Wickit. He started to tease Clara about how concerned she had looked, adding that perhaps they should make it a double wedding!

Trying hard to redeem herself, Clara told Wickit to go, or Melissa would be after him! Her face was as red as a beetroot. Everyone laughed. After Wickit disappeared for the second time, Clara told the twins that they should go to Tom's to find out why Melissa had sent the message.

As always, Tom was only too pleased to see them. He told Clara that he had been given an invitation to the Royal wedding, adding that he felt quite honoured, although he couldn't really understand why he had been asked. Clara blushed and quickly changed the subject by asking Tom why they were told to visit him. He explained that Melissa had sent something for the twins. "For us?" piped Jamie. "What is it?" "Foller me," said Tom, "it's in the barn!" As they followed Tom across his yard, Jamie kept asking what it was. "Look for yaself." said Tom, as he opened the barn door. "WOW!" gasped the twins. "Are they for us?" Jokingly, Tom replied, "Well, I don' imagine for one minute, that they're for me an' your Aunt Clara." Directly in front of them were two shiny new bikes. "Fantastic!" yelled Jamie, as he climbed on his. "Yeah that's the one, top of the range!" "'Old on a minute," said Tom, "there's somethin' else," "What! For us?" asked Maddy. "Yep, just foller me." The twins followed Tom towards the rear of the barn. Suddenly, Maddy spotted the two ponies. Unable to contain her excitement, she rushed towards them. "Oh Aunt Clara, I've got a pony!" Looking at her niece, Clara simply said, "You deserve it my dear!" Both ponies were identical, pure white, one male one female. Maddy hugged the pony round the neck. "Oh, he's so beautiful." What are ya goin' to call 'im?"asked Tom. Without hesitation, Maddy replied, "STAR!" "Good name," said Tom. "What 'bout your pony Jamie?" Thinking for a brief moment, Jamie replied, "DANCER!" "Another good choice," said Tom. "I think yer Aunt Clara and I will leave ya two 'ere and p'raps we'll go an' 'ave a cuppa." "What a good idea," smiled Clara, adding to the twins to be careful. Although she need not have worried, because both of them were good riders, having had lessons back home.

CHAPTER TWENTY-SEVEN

The Royal Wedding

Tom arrived at Clara's. "My, you do look smart!" said Clara, as she opened the door and looked at him. Appearing rather nervous and fumbling with his tie, Tom explained to her that he hadn't worn a suit in probably twenty years. "Well you look very smart," said Clara, adding that they should be leaving, as they didn't really want to be late for the Royal wedding.

Artex was waiting for them in the forest. Tom was shaking slightly; this truly was a big day for him, never having been to a fairy village before. He was quite mesmerized as he entered the village. Artex took them to a huge marquee, which had been made from pure silk and was only used on the most special of occasions. Inside, the tables were laid with the most beautiful flowers you could ever imagine. Soft music drifted along on the breeze; the royal horn blowers stood silently, waiting to announce the arrival of the King. Tables full of food lined the edges of the marquee, a stunning array of delicacies. Fruits in every conceivable shape and colour cascaded from golden bowls. A fairy orchestra sat patiently waiting to play; wine flowed freely from a lily fountain. Breathtaking was the word that Clara used to describe it, as they were shown to their table. It was directly in front of the Royal table. Tom confided in Clara that he would have been far happier at the back.

Suddenly the horns sounded. Everyone rose to their feet. A breathtaking hush followed, as the King entered with the beautiful Princess Melissa, proudly clutching her father's arm. Following behind them was Princess Michelalena and Princess Bellaruth, who both looked equally beautiful. Behind them came three small fairy children, each carrying a basket of flower petals, which they were throwing onto the ground as they passed the tables. Last, but by no means least, came Nanamic, escorted by Prince Iandrew. He was dressed in a military style tunic, complete with his sword which shone like new silver.

As they reached the centre of the room, everyone took their places. It was very different from a traditional human wedding where the groom arrives first. Princess Melissa stood in front of the King with her family and the flower maids to either side of her. She looked absolutely stunning with a white tunic style dress. A garland of flowers hung around her neck, tiny bands of flowers hung from her beautiful golden hair. Her eyes sparkled like two large crystals. Jamie could not take his eyes off her, so much so that his sister had to nudge him to bring him back to reality. Suddenly, the horns played again. Everyone watched as Wickit entered. As always, his trusty friend Artex was by his side. What a handsome pair they were, in their military tunics complete with swords. Wickit wore a garland of flowers around his head. He looked up towards Melissa, his mouth dropped open. Never before, had he looked upon anyone or anything as beautiful. King Peteron conducted the service. As he finished, the room erupted into cheering and clapping; finally they were husband and wife! Clara whispered to the others, that this was indeed a fairy tale with a happy ending.

CHAPTER TWENTY-EIGHT

Going Home

"Have you checked that you haven't left anything?" asked Clara, as the twins brought their suitcases downstairs. "I've double checked the room," replied Maddy. "I'll miss you both so terribly," said a sad looking Clara. "Likewise," quipped Jamie, "but before you know it, we'll be back. I'm sure mum and dad will let us return, even if they can't get away. "Tom's here," said Maddy. "It's nice of him to drive us to the airport." "Are we all ready?" asked Tom, as he entered Clara's kitchen. "I believe so," replied Clara. "Good, 'cos I need to make a quick detour," said Tom.

Everyone was quiet as they drove along in Tom's truck, except for Jamie, who wanted to know where they were going. "Well, I thought it wouldn' be quite right goin' back to the States without sayin' goodbye to Apple an' the ponies. "Oh thank you Tom" said Maddy, near to tears. Time passed quickly at the farm. The twins told the animals that they would be back in no time and that Tom and Aunt Clara would take really good care of them. "Children, we really must leave now or you'll miss your flight." Kissing the animals goodbye, they returned to Tom's truck.

At the airport, a familiar face greeted them. It was Janet, the stewardess. "How lovely to see you all again. Did you have a good holiday?" "The best!" said Jamie. "Oh, that's our flight just being announced, we must board now." Giving Aunt Clara and Tom a hug, the twins walked away with Janet. Just as they were about to wave goodbye, Janet stopped. "I forgot to tell your aunt something," she said, as she turned and returned to Clara. Leaning towards her, Janet whispered to her that Cynthia had indeed made a full recovery much to everyone's amazement. With a grin all over her face, Clara simply said that she never doubted for one moment that she wouldn't!

Clara and Tom waited until the plane had taken off. Clara told Tom how much she would miss the twins; she looked decidedly sad. Gently, Tom squeezed her hand and said "Don' fret Clara, they'll be back 'afore we know it, although I don' think any of us will ferget this holiday in an 'urry." "That's for sure," smiled Clara. "It truly has been one magical summer."

Printed in the United Kingdom
by Lightning Source UK Ltd.
124392UK00002B/192/A